KT-559-333

SHADOW OF GUILT

It starts out as a simple mission to trace his kid brother, but Brad Caulderfield rides into trouble when he kills the brother of Marshal Seth Blevins. Charged with murder and pursued by the lawman, Brad has to run for his life. He faces further complications from Stella Goodnight, who is out for his blood when he fails to return her affections. And when his brother reappears, bearing bitter resentments, he is looking headlong into the face of his nemesis . . .

Books by Mark Bannerman
in the Linford Western Library:

ESCAPE TO PURGATORY
THE EARLY LYNCHING
MAN WITHOUT A YESTERDAY
THE BECKONING NOOSE
GRAND VALLEY FEUD
RENEGADE ROSE
TRAIL TO REDEMPTION
COMANCHERO RENDEZVOUS
THE PINKERTON MAN
RIDE INTO DESTINY
GALVANIZED YANKEE
RAILROADED!
THE FRONTIERSMAN
LUST TO KILL
HOG-TIED HERO
BLIND TRAIL
BENDER'S BOOT
LEGACY OF LEAD
FURY AT TROON'S FERRY
GUNSMOKE AT ADOBE WALLS
THE MAVERICKS

MARK BANNERMAN

SHADOW OF GUILT

Complete and Unabridged

LINFORD
Leicester

First published in Great Britain in 2012 by
Robert Hale Limited
London

First Linford Edition
published 2014
by arrangement with
Robert Hale Limited
London

A catalogue record for this book is available
from the British Library.

ISBN 978–1–4448–1956–4

Published by
F. A. Thorpe (Publishing)
Anstey, Leicestershire

Set by Words & Graphics Ltd.
Anstey, Leicestershire
Printed and bound in Great Britain by
T. J. International Ltd., Padstow, Cornwall

This book is printed on acid-free paper

This book is dedicated to my wife
Françoise
Who supported me through the
dark days

1

They had thick, black bodies with yellow bellies and heads that were large and blunt-snouted — water snakes. They were known as cottonmouths because when they opened their jaws they displayed a gaping cotton-coloured mouth that harboured their venom-delivering fangs. Right now a score of snakes was entwined to form a seething ball, a dark, almost indiscernible shadow beneath the surface of Devil's Creek. The slow current embraced them, carrying them downstream towards the ford.

A mile away Brad Caulderfield heeled greater speed into his jaded appaloosa mare as they descended the twisting trail towards the ford, but despite never breaking her long stride she was not a fast horse. Frequently he risked a backward glance, fearful that he would glimpse the chasing posse; however his view was obscured by the steep, mesquite-cloaked banks which rose on each side of the trail. But instinct warned him that his pursuers were gaining on him.

Overhead, the afternoon sun was a huge fireball that he felt was broiling his brains. Yet even now his mind wrestled with the nightmare events that had occurred during the last forty-eight hours: *forty-eight hours in which he had killed a man*.

Seven months ago a row had flared between Brad's father and his kid brother Lanny. The cause had been Lanny's irresponsibility. When he should have been attending to his smallholding work, feeding the pigs, chickens, erecting fences and helping to build the new barn, he had been away. They suspected that he was in town, gambling, drinking and whoring, not caring a damn.

Old William Caulderfield had wind-seamed, leathery features with shaggy brows, and he was badly crippled in the left leg. A Union mini-ball had smashed his knee at the Battle of Shiloh. The limb might have been amputated but it never was; fortunately it had not become gangrenous, but ever since he had been obliged to use a crutch to limp around. To run the smallholding he needed the help of his sons and Dan Carter, a loyal Negro who had been employed by them for ten years.

Their home was a sizable spread on Chippers Creek, six miles west of Summerton, Texas. When he was twenty Brad had found happiness. He had courted and married the preacher's copper-haired daughter — eighteen-year-old Mary-Ellen. He was delighted by her calm acceptance of him in the marriage bed, and she, in turn, found in him a powerful sanctuary, a refuge from the harshness of frontier life. They had moved into a log-built cabin five miles from his father's home — a cabin with strong walls and a cheery hearth. They had been blessed by the birth of a daughter whom they named Betsy.

Mary-Ellen had a happy, bright nature but she was afraid of Lanny, seeing an evil violence lingering in his dark eyes. She avoided him whenever she could. It wasn't always easy because, taking the baby, she went up to the smallholding every day to clean the house, do the washing and cook meals.

When Lanny had returned from his overnight carousal an exchange of angry words erupted. The result was that Lanny had struck his father across the cheek, knocking him back into his chair. Brad had jumped to intervene, pushing his brother away.

'One day soon,' Lanny had yelled, 'I'll come back an' I'll kill you both!' Then he stormed out of their homestead, his face mottled with rage. Suddenly they heard the roar of a pistol and, rushing to the open doorway, Brad saw their old dog lying motionless, his blood forming a rivulet on the wooden planking of the veranda.

'Lanny's killed Roamer,' Brad stated.

For a long moment his father was silent. Eventually he said, 'Lanny'll come back sooner rather than later.' His cheek was bloody where Lanny's chunky ring had cut him. He bowed his head and wiped away a tear.

Later that day, Brad had buried old Roamer.

Six months had elapsed with no word from Lanny.

Strangely, the old man still harboured a long-suffering love for his youngest son, seemingly forgetting all his callous ways. Soon, not a day passed when he didn't mutter his grief. Maybe he saw Lanny's shortcomings as a reflection of his own parental failure. He had promised, on his wife's deathbed, that he would care for both their sons. But Brad didn't share his sentiments, thinking them to be misguided. He had been glad enough to see the back of his brother, no longer to have to suffer the black moods and constant, smouldering resentment that Lanny exuded.

And then came another morning that neither of them would ever forget.

Brad was up at the main homestead, taking a break from chopping wood, drinking strong black coffee with his father, when they heard the rattle of an approaching wagon. They both walked out on to the veranda, shading their eyes against the sun. After a moment the old man said, 'It's Major Mulvaney! An' he's got his daughter with him. What can they want at this time o' day?'

The springboard wagon was coming at a fair pace, bouncing up and down over the rugged trail. It was brought to a dust-swirling halt in front of the house.

Mulvaney owned the Bar-B ranch, which covered a vast acreage that took in all the surrounding country. He owned the land on which the Caulderfield homesteads stood and had leased it out to the family for years. There had never been any trouble but now Brad felt uneasy.

The rancher was an upright man. His

long waving hair and beard were white, as were the brows beetling over his piercing eyes. Right now his face was an angry red. He dwarfed his seventeen-year-old daughter Lilith who sat, bonneted head down, beside him on the wagon.

'Howdy, Major,' William Caulderfield called. 'Come in for a coffee.'

'To hell with coffee!' Mulvaney responded. He rammed on the brake and climbed down from the wagon. 'I'm gonna talk to you, Caulderfield, and what I say ain't gonna be good to hear. I'm comin' inside where it's cooler.' He turned to his daughter. 'Come on, Lilith. You're gonna tell exactly what happened.'

The girl climbed from the far side of the wagon and walked round to join her father. She kept her eyes downcast and Brad noticed how she was trembling. She was just a slip of a girl, with a touch of her Mexican mother about her. They all trooped in to the shadowed interior of the homestead's

7

parlour. When they were all seated, Mulvaney spoke in an angry voice.

'It's your boy, Lanny.'

'What about him? He left here six months ago,' William Caulderfield said. 'We ain't seen hide nor hair of him since.'

'Well, he didn't go far,' Mulvaney went on. 'He camped out somewhere on my range and spent his time havin' his way with Lilith. Ain't that so, gal?'

Without raising her head, Lilith's murmur came almost inaudibly. 'Yes, Pa.'

'An' I didn't know anythin' about it,' the rancher stormed, 'not till yesterday. Not even her ma knew. We thought she was out ridin' with her Mexican friend. Well, apparently Lanny got rough with her, treating her like a whore! Maybe she didn't deserve nothin' better, but that ain't the point. Anyway, I got suspicious. I tracked her and ended up near where Lanny had made camp in a swale. That was where I found them. When he saw me, Lanny drew his gun.

He was so mad. He waved his gun at me, then fired a shot over my head. After that he ran off to where he had his horse tethered. He mounted up an' galloped away hell for leather. I went to Lilith an' . . . well, you tell them what he'd done to you.'

The girl suddenly burst into tears: long, raking sobs.

Her father showed her no compassion. 'Fact is I'm downright ashamed of what she's been up to. My own kin deceivin' me — an' now she's payin' for it!' He turned to her. 'Cut out the sob-stuff, Lilith. Tell them what he did to you.'

The girl seemed to take hold of herself although her voice was still little more than a whisper and there was a flush rising in her cheeks. 'He raped me.' She paused, swallowing hard, then she continued. 'He used to read me poetry. It was so good, but last time he . . . raped me.' She rested her arms on the table and dropped her head on to her arms, shuddering with silent tears.

In that moment the only sound was the raspy breathing of the menfolk.

Then Mulvaney issued his ultimatum. 'I want Lanny back here an' I want him put on trial; then I want him shut away or, better still, strung up. I'll give you three months to bring him back. If he ain't here by then, every Caulderfield will be off my land, homesteads an' all!'

He didn't say any more. He reached for the girl's hand and half-dragged her back outside.

Brad and his father sat, tight-jawed, in stunned silence as they heard the wagon depart.

For the next week his father had gazed out from the homestead across the Texas landscape, hoping, praying, to see a horseman who, as he approached, would become recognizable as Lanny, coming back to face judgment for his sins.

'It was all my fault,' the old man sighed, his teeth grating against his pipe-stem in anguish. 'I should've brought him up better. If Ma was still alive she'd have kept him on the straight and narrow.'

Brad nodded. It had been a crippling blow to the small family when his mother had developed complications following an attack of measles and died, three years since. Hers had been the warmth that made home into a loving place. She left a grief-stricken widower and two sons aged nineteen and sixteen.

Now, Brad saw his father's depression increasing every day. Unless Lanny came back they would face eviction.

'What can we do, son? I guess Lanny won't come back of his own accord.'

Brad broached the subject that perhaps he ought to have raised before. 'Pa, mebbe I should go look for Lanny.'

'It's a big world out there,' the old man said. 'He could be in Mexico by now.'

'I might be able to pick up some clue,' Brad was full of doubts; he shared his father's misery. But he tried to put confidence into his words. 'He might be nearer than we think. I guess you and Dan can keep this place runnin' for a few weeks.'

His father pondered for a while, then he said, 'If you go, make sure you come back safe. I couldn't stand losin' two sons.'

'I won't look for trouble, Pa. I'll just ask around for Lanny. Somebody must know where he is.'

The old man sighed again, but he nodded. 'Six weeks, that's all. After that, you come home, whether you found him or not, understand?'

'Sure, Pa.' Brad paused, then added, 'I'll leave tomorrow mornin'.'

Of course the situation was fraught with uncertainty. Even if he did find Lanny, he wasn't going to surrender meekly and come back to face the music. But that was something Brad would have to deal with if and when he did track his brother down.

That afternoon Brad spoke to the Negro Dan Carter and explained to

12

him what was happening. He asked Dan if Annie, his wife, would stay with Mary-Ellen while he was away as he did not like leaving her alone. Dan immediately nodded. 'She'd sure love that.'

Before dawn next day Brad had packed his saddle-bags with the few necessities he would need, together with the carefully wrapped trail food of fried prairie chicken, boiled ham, biscuits and assorted pies that his wife had prepared, then he strapped on his blue-steel Colt .45 and kissed Mary-Ellen and the baby farewell. Mary-Ellen lifted her tearful eyes to his, her features softened by the early-morning lamp-light, her lissom body pressed to his. 'I sure hope you never have to use that gun, honey,' she murmured. 'I'm so scared you'll run into a heap o' trouble. Betsy and I couldn't stand life without you. I'll pray for you every night.'

He had calmed her with more kisses and assurances that he felt at the time were justified, after which he rode away on his appaloosa mare Nelly with a vision of his wife's loving face in his mind.

Brad was a well built twenty-two years old, his muscles hardened by work on the homestead which he had never shirked, turning the soil with their old plough, raising crops, building fences and tending livestock. He was halfway handsome, with a fine, straight nose. Before Mary-Ellen had come into his life, he had enjoyed his regular trips to Summerton, proving himself a fair hand at saloon poker, though he never gambled beyond his means, nor drank whiskey in excess, nor often consorted with whores. Marriage had changed him into a sober, faithful and God-fearing husband.

By four weeks after he had left home, Brad had done the rounds of most of the townships and ranches within a radius of fifty miles, asking over and over if anybody had seen his brother, hopeful that the unusual name of Caulderfield might strike a cord. He had asked in stores, saloons, hotels, town marshals' offices, brothels and even in morgues. But the response was always the same — a blank face and a shake of the head. And then, finally, he rode into Buffalo Springs.

Never, in his wildest dreams, had he imagined that he would shortly encounter Mary-Ellen's worst fears: that he would gun a man down and be charged with his murder!

And now, these fleeting, chaotic hours later, he reached Devil's Ford and burst through the phalanx of cottonwoods that lined the bank. The water of the creek glinted in the blistering sunlight, half-blinding him. The heaving appaloosa hesitated, then gallantly splashed forward, finding the depth greater than anticipated.

They were two-thirds of the way across when suddenly the horse unleashed an agonized scream, reared up, then plunged back in an eruption of water. Glancing down, Brad saw a mass of black bodies swirling just below the surface like a multitude of worms. Simultaneously he felt sharp pain lance up from the calf of his left leg. As the panicking appaloosa staggered forward he half-fell from her back but, clinging to the saddle horn, he restored his upright position. He realized that a snake was hanging with its jaws clamped to his leg. With an almighty thrash of his arm he bludgeoned it away.

With supreme effort the mare reached the far bank, her forelegs punctured with bites. As venom pulsed through her veins, she went down, firstly on her knees, then she rolled over, crushing Brad. Stunned, he lay for minutes scarcely making sense of what had happened, conscious of the horse's rattling breath. Then realization dawned on him and, cursing over and over, he heaved himself out from beneath the quivering animal. He staggered to his feet but his legs buckled and he dropped, aware that his body was raked with pain.

2

'What'll we do when we catch him, Marshal?' stumpy, bespectacled Kenny Tolly enquired in his slow, sing-song voice. He was a simple-minded soul whose naivety was suffered by his companions with varying degrees of impatience.

The posse of Marshal Seth Blevins, a big, red-faced man with a drooping moustache that made him look permanently mournful, and six deputies had reined in their horses at the point where the trail forked. Walking Hawk, the Kickapoo Indian, had dismounted to check the tracks on the arid ground.

'Reckon he head for creek,' he said, straightening up. He climbed back into his saddle. He was slightly inebriated.

'He ain't far ahead now, that's for sure,' the marshal grunted. His mood was a mixture of ferment and anger.

His brother had been murdered and he didn't take kindly to it. He removed his hat and wiped the sweat from his brow with his forearm.

'What'll we do when we catch him?' Kenny Tolly repeated. 'I guess I'd string him up to the nearest tree if he'd killed my brother.'

'We'll hang the sonofabitch all right,' Seth Blevins growled, ramming his hat back on. 'Only I want to skin him alive first!'

'Need a sharp knife for that,' Tolly commented.

Soon they were pounding forward again, heading towards the ford, their blood up in the knowledge that they were closing on their prey.

* * *

A mile away, across Devil's Creek, Brad Caulderfield's appaloosa mare Nelly had succumbed to water-snake venom and breathed her last.

Dazedly, Brad fumbled to remove the

crimson bandanna from his throat. He was in the cotton-woods that lined the creek. He knew that he had to establish a ligature before blood and lymph carried the venom into his circulation. His hands were shaking as he drew the bandanna around above his boot-top and knotted it tightly. He pulled the leg of his Levis up, cursing as he saw the single puncture in his calf from which a trickle of blood was showing. A dent in the leather indicated where a second puncture had been shielded by the stovepipe boot. Even so, his leg was swelling. Thoughts of attempting to suck out the poison came to him, but his strength was failing and he was not a contortionist.

He tried to move, but a slow, heavy coldness was spreading through his body. His vision was blurred and he was seeing double. He could make out two appaloosas lying motionless a few yards away, though he knew there was only one. He felt grief at having lost his horse. Already blowflies were settling on the dead animal, like a shimmering metallic blanket. Brad's breathing was becoming shallow, as if a tight band encircled his chest. Bile rose in his throat and he vomited. He slumped back on the earth, feeling that he was close to death. He didn't care if Marshal Blevins caught him now, but then he remembered Mary-Ellen's heart-felt words: *Betsy and I couldn't stand life without you.* He drifted into unconsciousness.

⋆　⋆　⋆

As the posse made haste around the twists and turns of the trail something weird happened; they heard a strange roaring sound that seemed to emanate from a low cloud above. It became so loud that the posse drew rein once more.

'I ain't never heard no cloud make that noise,' Deputy Tom Evans gasped.

They gazed skywards, their mouths open in amazement — then within seconds their mouths were closed and the mystery was explained, because the cloud was breaking up, great fragments sweeping down towards the ground.

'It's damned grasshoppers — masses of 'em!' The marshal shouted to make himself heard above the roar which had increased to deafening proportions. The air was throbbing with the beat of millions of wings. The horses tossed their heads, neighing frantically, rearing in panic. Kenny Tolly was thrown from his saddle, and his glasses were smashed amid chopping hoofs. The sky had darkened, the light was diminishing. Soon the men were using their hats in a vain bid to beat off the fluttering bugs, struggling to snatch breath in the thickening atmosphere, and simultaneously fighting to control their terrified animals.

Like hail, the grasshoppers were slamming into the men, horses, ground and all else in their path — coating everything with their heaped bodies, turning the world into a seething nightmare.

As one man, the posse swung from their saddles, coughing and gasping as they sought shelter behind their horses. Kenny Tolly spluttered and choked. When he breathed in, he sucked an insect into his mouth, which he promptly swallowed. Everybody now fastened their bandannas over their faces. Walking Hawk, who was not wearing boots but moccasins, felt grasshoppers crawling up inside his Levis; he cried out and attempted to crush them before they reached his vitals.

In the six miles behind them the plague of creatures chomped everything they touched. They even devoured clothes that were hanging on lines. Trying to save crops was futile and plants were denuded to their stalks. Grasshoppers found their way into barns and chewed on harnesses and hoe-handles. In Buffalo Springs they invaded houses, settling on tables and chairs, clinging to curtains and beds. At every step they were crunched underfoot but still more came.

For six hours the insects continued to

swarm. The men of the posse were slumped on the ground, their bodies covered with the creatures. Three horses, including the marshal's, broke free and fled back towards town. Another collapsed, soon to be buried beneath grasshoppers.

And then, as if from nowhere, a bullying wind arose, and within twenty minutes it had swept the air clean of the pests, sending them on to plague some other district. It was beginning to get dark. The posse members rose, removing their bandannas and brushing themselves clear of insect bodies. Kenny Tolly groped around unable, to see without his glasses. The remaining horses were in a bad way and would be of little use.

'What are we gonna do, Marshal?' buck-toothed Josh Tomlinson enquired. 'I ain't never seen nothin' like that!'

Marshal Blevins scowled as he surveyed his surroundings. The ground was littered with bugs. He walked a few paces, crushing bodies beneath his boots. The state of the horses was depressing.

One was sprawled on its side, its breath heaving in painful surges, its eyes showing bloodshot whites. It appeared to be in the throes of dying.

'I guess best we can do is head back to town,' the marshal said. 'The sonofabitch who killed my brother is probably miles away by now, if he survived the grasshoppers. It'll be night mighty soon and we'll never find him, not if we're on foot. We'll have another search tomorrow. I ain't gonna give up on him. Nobody guns down a Blevins and gets away with it.'

There was a general agreement and a relief that they were going back to Buffalo Springs. With their horses unridable they had a wearisome walk ahead of them, but that was better than pushing blindly on.

'Better shoot that hoss,' Kenny Tolly said.

The marshal nodded. Tolly drew one of his pistols, peered close and dispatched the poor beast, seeming to take a delight in the task.

3

Nobody could explain, or even try to explain, why the great swirling mass of grasshoppers did not spread across the creek but swung north towards Buffalo Springs. Brad Caulderfield recovered his senses unaware of the plague that had caused such havoc. His mind wrestled to recall the events that had left him sprawled on the ground on the bank of the creek. He realized it was dark. He also realized that he was not dead. He must have been unconscious for hours. He suddenly noticed the prostrate bulk of his mare, pale in the gloom, stretched out a few yards from him, and grim realization came to him. Where were his pursuers? Why hadn't they found him? Had the snakes got them too? Whatever had happened, he could not stay where he was.

As he attempted to sit up pain

throbbed up from his leg and through his body, causing him to emit a despairing cry. He felt bruised all over from the crushing he'd suffered beneath Nelly. The nightmare vision of the cottonmouth clinging with jaws clamped to his leg, tormented him, and to ensure that it was not still there he jerked his arm to brush it away. The movement brought a renewed spasm of pain. A horned toad was observing him with sombre eyes, just feet away. It moved off as he stirred.

Gritting his teeth, he pressed his hands on to the ground and forced himself into a sitting position. He wondered if venom was pulsing through his veins. Why had he so far survived when the mare, far bigger than he, had succumbed?

His senses were clearing. His body felt cold and he could not stop his teeth from chattering. He concentrated on drawing air into his lungs; presently he forced himself on to his feet, tottering at first but then gaining confidence. His glance again went to Nelly and he groaned at the loss of his loyal mount.

His awareness was drawn back to his leg. He could feel that the swelling extended to above his knee. He checked the tourniquet and untied it, then restored it, drawing it tighter. How long would it be before he suffered the same fate as the appaloosa? He placed his weight on the punctured leg and found that it supported him. He recalled once more the last words that Mary-Ellen had spoken, and a determination seemed to flow through him. But one thing appeared certain: unless he got medical attention, some antidote to snake poison, he would most likely die. His brain groped with possibilities.

When he had ridden down the main street of Buffalo Springs two days ago, he had noticed a signboard proclaiming the partnership of two medical practitioners. If he could get back to town, keeping himself as inconspicuous as possible, he might be able to get treatment that would eradicate the venom from his system. He could certainly pay well for it. He still had the wad of money bulging his pocket that he had won at the saloon poker table. It seemed that going back to Buffalo Springs was risking his neck, but there wasn't another town or doctor within miles, and provided he could avoid the marshal and his deputies he had a chance of staying clear of trouble. In his dazed state his reasoning might not have been sound, but he made his decision and he determined, provided his legs supported him, to attempt the walk, difficult as it would be.

But there was one hurdle he had to surmount first. The ford had to be recrossed and the fear was in him that the snakes might still be lingering. He wished he could bury the horse and also that he could carry his saddle with him, but he hadn't the strength for either task. However, he went to his saddle-bag, unbuckled it and drew out his canvas coat and what food he had left from his purchase in Buffalo

Springs. He rolled up his coat and placed it on his shoulder. He unfastened his gunbelt and hung it around his neck.

Fear caused him to pause as he gazed at the water of the ford. It reflected the sickle of the moon. He tried to peer beneath the surface, tried in vain to determine that the way was clear of snakes. Taking a gamble, he waded in. Within four paces, the water rose to his waist, icy cold. He was sure something touched his leg and in sudden fright he hurried on, almost falling. He reached the far bank and breathed a sigh of relief. The lower part of his body was dripping wet. He strapped his gunbelt in place. He removed the coat from his shoulder and struggled in to it. At least it was dry. He hobbled forward, passing through the deep shadow of cottonwoods that lined the creek.

Soon he was clear of the trees, climbing the rising, twisting trail. His leg was paining him with every step, but he gritted his teeth and tried to ignore it. Presently he became aware of something crunching beneath his boots. He crouched down, fumbled with his hands. At first he was puzzled, then he grunted with surprise as he realized that the ground was littered with the bodies of dead grasshoppers, But he did not meditate on it; he straightened up and pressed on.

Weakness still hampered him and he paused frequently to rest his leg. He felt it was trying to burst clear of his constricting boot. Overhead, the thin moon provided little light, and the stars seemed high and remote. Once, he saw a shooting star scratch its fire across the heavens. He heard the hoot of a ground-owl and later on the howl of a wolf that was answered from surprisingly close by. Alongside the trail cactus loomed, forming weird, ghostly shapes.

After what seemed an age he reached the point where the trail forked. He covered a further mile, then he slumped down, overcome by pain and weakness. In him was the forlorn feeling that he was not going to make it to Buffalo Springs. He had been foolish to think he could. He wondered if he might die before the dawn. He thought about Lanny and cursed him. Why had he taken it into his head to disappear off the face of the earth? Maybe he was dead. He associated his brother with the snakes, wondering if they were somehow a reincarnation of him, driven to inject poison into those he hated. Brad realized that his brain was wandering. He rested back on the ground. Maybe he would sleep for a little while, regain his strength.

He had no idea how long he slumbered, but he awoke feeling stiff and cold. His Levis remained damp and his leg still throbbed with pain. Again he felt it imperative to reach a doctor if he was to survive. Even now it might be too late. He felt wretched. He glanced up and saw that the stars and moon had gone and the sky showed a paleness. He clambered up, setting his feet in motion once more, heading onward along the trail. He did not know how many miles he had covered, but he felt certain he still had a good way to go.

Dawn was brightening the eastern heavens when he again rested. He ate the food he had with him, but it made him feel sick. He wondered if he could go on. It would be so easy to give in and welcome whatever the next world had to offer. He lay back. Just doze for a while, he told himself. He closed his eyes, soon fell asleep. He dreamed of Mary-Ellen. She was baking bread in the cabin's kitchen.

★ ★ ★

'Wake up! Wake up, *señor*!' A hand slapped his face. It was as if he was still dreaming. He opened his eyes and blinked in the bright sunshine and realized that the man stooping over him was not part of a dream. His breath smelt of pulque. 'Wake up, *señor*,' the words came again. 'Too much whiskey, eh?'

'No . . . not drinkin',' Brad mumbled. 'Snakebite.' His eyes focused on the stranger. He was clearly a Mexican, maybe in his thirties, wearing a wide straw sombrero. He had a swarthy face that was the colour of tallow and a wilted, straggly moustache.

'Snakebite. *Madre de Dios*!'

Brad saw how his front teeth were badly chipped. He noticed that behind this man was a four-wheeled camp-wagon pulled by a single dapple-grey horse, drawn up on the trail.

'I have to get to a doc,' he said.

'*Sí, señor*. I go to Buffalo Springs. I take you . . . if you 'ave money.'

Brad scrambled to his feet. 'Yeah . . . I'll pay you.' He was swaying slightly, his grogginess persisting.

'You get in back of wagon,' the Mexican instructed. 'You'd fall off the front seat.' Grasping Brad's elbow, he guided him to the rear of the wagon and helped him clamber in. Brad seated himself amongst an assortment of parcels. He reckoned he would have to be careful when he reached Buffalo Springs to keep out of sight as much as possible.

His benefactor, whose name was Carlos Bautista, pulled himself up on to the front seat, let the brake off, took hold of the lines and set the iron-tyred wagon in jolting motion. 'I hurry,' he said. 'I 'ave parcels to deliver to marshal.'

4

Marshal Seth Blevins was in a sour mood. He left home early, partly to escape the acid tongue of his sister, Hanna, with whom he lived in the guest house that she ran, and partly because he had a lot to think about. He had to arrange his brother Frank's funeral. But most important, he had somehow to track down Frank's murderer, and right now he didn't have a lot to go on. He didn't have his name. Admittedly, he would recognize him if he saw him, but for that he had to get within seeing distance and the man could be a hundred miles away by now.

'What're you gonna do about catchin' that devil who gunned down our dear brother?' Hanna had nagged as she dumped his breakfast of hoe cake, beans and eggs in front of him. 'It's no good sitting on your ass!' She had a black mole at the corner of her mouth and a nose red enough to light a fire with. She had never shown much affection for Frank when he was alive but now he had assumed the character of a saint in her mind. On reflection, she had never shown much affection to anybody, but constantly sought things about which she could nag or complain. Frank had spent most of his time drinking whiskey or indulging his craving for whores. He had been something of an embarrassment to his brother, the marshal. But killing a Blevins was not something that could be ignored.

'We'd've got him if it hadn't been for those damned grasshoppers,' Blevins claimed. 'But I'll track him down if it's the last thing I do.' He got up, leaving half his breakfast, and stomped along the sidewalk to his office.

Buffalo Springs had one main street which was twenty metres wide and lined with stores, two hotels, three boarding houses, three saloons, a

Gothic-styled church and a bank. It also boasted a courthouse, a lawyer's office and the medical practitioners' surgery.

When Blevins reached his office, Kenny Tolly was outside sweeping grasshoppers off the sidewalk. He was wearing his two ivory-butted Colt .45s, a brocaded vest and chaps decorated with conchas and a wide-brimmed Stetson. He was done up as if he was the greatest gunfighter the West had ever known, but in truth he was a comical figure.

'We gonna catch that killer today, Marshal?' he enquired brightly, squinting through his wire-rimmed replacement spectacles which he'd purchased at the mercantile store for a week's wages. Blevins gave him a scowl, unlocked his office door and went in. He was seething with anger.

He worked for an hour, shuffling through some paperwork, after which he decided to go and see the local minister to fix Frank's burying. He left

Kenny Tolly in charge of the office. Tolly puffed out his chest and sat down in the marshal's chair.

★ ★ ★

The sun was well up in the sky, the heat taking hold, when the Mexican Carlos Bautista drove his wagon into town. Brad Caulderfield had paid him generously for the transport and the assurance that he would deliver him to the doctors' surgery and not talk about it thereafter. But the Mexican was not a man of honour. Despite his promise, he had decided to inform the marshal about the man he had conveyed to town. There might be a few dollars more in it for him.

The wagon drew up outside the surgery. Brad noticed the plate proclaiming *Dr Murphy MD & Dr Wilson MD, Medical practitioners*. He dropped from the back of the wagon, expressed his thanks to Bautista, climbed on to the sidewalk and rang the bell. There was no response so he opened the door and hobbled into the shadowy interior. After the brightness of the sun he had difficulty in seeing. When his vision cleared it was to observe a man in an Aberdeen coat emerging from an inner room.

'Good morning, sir. What can I do for you?' this man said. He was a tall, lantern-jawed individual with a shock of red hair and rosy-cheeks, and from the Irish twang in his voice Brad guessed he was Doc Murphy.

'Snakebite,' Brad got out. 'I've been bitten by a cottonmouth.'

'You better come this way.' The doc gestured to the doorway from which he had emerged. 'Get on the couch.'

A moment later Brad was sprawled back on a couch in what was obviously the combined surgery and pharmacy. On shelves lining the walls were jars of drugs, liniments, ointments, painkillers and pills.

After giving him a large drink of water the doctor removed his boot with several hard tugs. He unfastened the bandanna, the ligature that had remained in place. He nodded with approval. Then he got some scissors and cut Brad's Levis up to above the knee, displaying the swollen, discoloured leg and the ugly puncture. It had stopped seeping blood.

He picked up the stovepipe boot and examined the top of it. 'You were lucky,' he said. 'Your boot took half the bite. You only got a half dose of poison.'

Brad nodded, feeling relieved. But then it occurred to him that sprawled back on the couch without his boot, he was mighty helpless. If the marshal burst in brandishing a gun he wouldn't stand a chance. He just prayed that his arrival in town had gone unnoticed and that the Mexican would keep his mouth shut.

'You're fortunate,' the doctor said. 'I've just been involved with the development of a new procedure with something called a hypodermic syringe.'

'What's that?' Brad enquired. He'd always imagined medicine was mainly taking pills, but now he watched with apprehension as, from a shelf, Murphy reached down a glass tube with a plunger at one end and an evil-looking needle at the other. He unplugged the plunger with a *thwock* sound. Next, he found a small bottle and poured its thick contents into the cylinder. 'This is an anti-venine serum,' he explained. 'It's an antidote for snake venom.'

He replaced the plunger in the cylinder and turned towards Brad. 'Roll up your sleeve,' he said.

Brad hesitated. He didn't fancy this serum, nor that great long needle, but then he again thought of the marshal; he rolled back his sleeve and held his arm up, turning his head to one side so as not to see. 'This won't hurt as much as a snakebite,' the doctor reassured him. Brad felt a sharp stab of pain as the needle was jabbed home and the serum forced into him.

Afterwards, with a small knife, Murphy made several incisions around the bite, causing Brad to clench his teeth to avoid cursing. Murphy then mixed and sponged on a solution, explaining that it was permanganate of potash, which sounded like a foreign language to Brad. After this, he bound up the wound with a bandage.

As the minutes ticked by Brad grew more anxious. Suddenly he tensed as he heard footsteps and another man entered the surgery. He was short and plump and had a sagging, fleshy-featured face. He nodded a greeting to Murphy. From his manner, Brad guessed that he was Doc Wilson, the other half of the medical partnership.

'He's been bitten by a cottonmouth,' Murphy explained, 'but I guess he'll survive.'

At first Wilson paid little attention to the patient on the couch. He was turning to leave when suddenly he swung back and gave Brad a long, hard look. His mouth drooped a little. He beckoned to his partner and the two men left the room. Brad heard the low murmur of their voices though he couldn't catch what they were saying. Alarm pulsed through his veins. He reached for his boot and with great effort pulled it on.

Just then the two men returned. Wilson looked at him and frowned.

'You must rest,' he said. 'That's if you want to recover. I'll give you something to help.' He reached for a bottle on the shelf, uncorked it and poured some of its contents into a small glass. 'Take this.' He handed the glass to Brad. 'Now I must go,' he added. 'I've got urgent business to attend to.' He left the surgery and the slam of the outer door sounded.

Brad still held the glass, but Murphy said, 'Don't take that! It'd put you to sleep for an hour.' He took the glass away. He swung back and added, 'You must get out of here quick. He recognized you!' He helped Brad to his feet. 'Leave through the back door and make yourself scarce.'

Brad stuffed ten dollars into Murphy's hand and hurriedly followed him down a hallway to the back door. 'Why're you helpin' me?' he gasped.

'I'm fed up with hangings in this town. I'm not here to certify folks dead. I'm here to cure them. Now for glory's sake *vamoose*!'

Brad nodded his gratitude and hobbled away.

★   ★   ★

Kenny Tolly sat in the marshal's chair, his fancy-booted feet on the desk, following the marshal's habit. He felt mighty important. He was looking at a newspaper, pretending he could read. He heard the wagon draw up outside and a moment later the Mexican Carlos Bautista rushed in. 'I need to tell Marshal Blevins somethin'!' he exclaimed.

'The marshal ain't here,' Tolly responded pompously. 'I'm in charge right now.'

'Where ees the marshal?'

'Oh, I dunno,' Tolly said. 'He don't

44

tell me everywhere he goes.'

'Well, I best wait for heem to come back,' the Mexican retorted. 'Meantime I get the parcels in.'

Tolly resumed looking at the newspaper while Bautista stacked the parcels in the corner of the office. Once this was done, he sat on top of them and waited impatiently. A half-hour passed and he was still waiting.

After a further fifteen minutes Doc Wilson rushed in, flustered with excitement, his bewhiskered face red. 'Where's the marshal?' he asked, and Tolly repeated that Blevins wasn't present right now, however he should be back soon.

But it was another half-hour before the marshal returned from fixing his brother's burying with the minister, who had been a difficult man to get away from, for he suffered from an excess of words.

* * *

When Brad quit the doctors' establishment, he realized that he was at the back of the buildings fronting Buffalo Springs's main street. He was about to rush on when he noticed the rear of the livery stable and a desperate idea came to him. Maybe he could get a horse and tack.

Glancing around to ensure the way was clear, he ran to the back entrance of the livery stable. Back and front, the doors were flung open. When he entered and looked up the runway he could see people and wagons passing along the main street. From there, anybody looking in would see him. He grunted anxiously. The stables were shadowy compared with the bright sunlight of the outside, but were lit by several oil lamps. The scent of horse ordure and nitrogen filled the air. He cast a swift glance around, seeing the horses, aware of his presence, blowing and moving restlessly in their stalls. Saddles were hanging on the rails.

'What d'you want, mister?' The

hostler, a humpbacked little man in a leather apron with a currycomb in his hand, had emerged from one of the stalls.

'I need a horse, a saddle and a sougan,' Brad got out, aggravated by the slow way the man spoke and moved.

The hostler scratched his jaw, then drawled, 'Fifteen dollars for the horse, forty for the saddle, five for the sougan. Cash on the nail.'

'Sure,' Brad nodded.

Ten minutes later he was astride a buckskin gelding that had a black mane and tail. The hostler assured him the animal was of good Spanish descent, but Brad was in no mood for discussing detail. He heeled the horse hard and they went out through the rear of the livery stable like a charge of canister, and into the wild terrain of mesquite trees, chaparral and shinnery oak, scaring an armadillo before them.

What he did not realize was that he had been spotted — not only spotted but recognized. Deputy Tom Evans had been passing along the street and had taken a casual glance through the open doorway of the livery. What he saw had him whipping out his gun and charging in — but he was too late to apprehend his quarry. Brad had vanished through the back exit. By the time Evans had followed up, he was nowhere to be seen.

Evans cursed and holstered his gun. He had to inform the marshal of events straight away. He was out in the street again when he met Blevins rushing from his abortive mission to the medical establishment. *He just got up and ran off*, Doc Murphy had explained. *I couldn't stop him.*

Now Evans blurted out his news and Blevins's eyes brightened. 'Mebbe we'll catch the sonofabitch now,' he gasped. He immediately dispatched Evans to fetch Walking Hawk, the Kickapoo.

Evans found Walking Hawk in his wickiup on the edge of town, drunk and trying to sleep it off. Evans shook him and gabbled out that the marshal wanted him. The Indian climbed unsteadily off his pallet, grabbed his canteen and, with the deputy leading the way, staggered to the livery where Blevins, already mounted, urged them to make haste.

While the tracker fumbled with his saddle, getting it on a horse at the third attempt, the hostler amplified the information that Evans had imparted. 'That fella didn't even stop for a bill of sale,' he concluded. There was no doubt in Blevins's mind. This man who had so far eluded them was definitely his brother's killer.

Once Walking Hawk was astride his horse the marshal led the way out through the rear of the livery in hot pursuit of the fugitive.

5

Lanny Caulderfield, Brad's kid brother, was well pleased with himself. He had just blasted open the strongbox with three shots from his Navy Colt. He had stolen the strongbox from the stagecoach he'd held up. He had also extracted a tidy sum in cash from the passengers, plus two gold watches, a pistol and a pearl necklace from the haughty woman on board.

Now the strongbox was open and he grinned with delight as he saw the neat wads of fifty-dollar bills inside. He was a wealthy man.

Lanny was safely ensconced in his hideout, deep in a remote canyon thirty miles north of Buffalo Springs. He had rigged up a shelter of woven ocotillo stalks piled with brush. It was as snug as any Apache wickiup; and close by, in a hole concealed by a slab of rock, was the cache where he would store the proceeds of his work. He lived off the game he snared, and he had built up a store of whiskey and other supplies from his discreet visits to the settlement of Silverwood, ten miles away.

His first hold-up had been surprisingly easy. He had watched the trail for days, spying out from a hiding place at the side. He noted the time and details of the stagecoach run. He knew that once each month the mining company pay roll was conveyed, accompanied by two heavily armed guards who rode behind the coach. He was not deterred by these. He was proud of his marksmanship with his new Winchester .44-calibre repeating rifle, which was capable of delivering fifteen rounds before reloading was necessary. For close up work he had his Navy Colt.

The gaily painted Concord coach, drawn by four horses, had appeared exactly on time, the two escorts riding with rifles slanted in front of them. There was also a shotgun messenger next to the driver. His heart pounding with excitement, Lanny watched them, keeping a bead on the taller of the escorts. When they were close he pressed the trigger, hitting his target squarely in the chest, throwing him back from his mount. As the second escort fumbled to raise his rifle, Lanny fired again, blasting the man from his saddle. His foot remained caught in his stirrup. The animal panicked, dragging the limp body along, until, finally, the man's foot came out of his boot and his body dropped to lie motionless on the trail while the horse charged on.

The coach driver had immediately lashed his horses into a gallop, but Lanny fired a third time, felling the off-side lead horse. The result was chaos. In a tangle of traces, the remaining animals staggered in a frenzy. One fell. The coach came to a shuddering halt, rocking on its leather thorough-braces but somehow remaining upright; the driver was thrown off his seat. As the man hit the ground and scrambled up, Lanny downed him with a shot to the lungs. The shotgun messenger had also fallen from his seat, but ran off into the trees on the far side.

Lanny smiled with satisfaction. He rose from his cover, pulling his bandanna over his face, and approached the stricken coach. The surviving horses struggled frantically in their snarled harness, snorting and trembling. With rifle at the ready, Lanny pulled open the door of the coach. Inside were two paunchy men in black frock coats and stewpot hats, and a haughty-faced woman. They all cowered back.

'Don't kill us,' one of the men pleaded. 'Take what you want.'

'Get out . . . stand on the road!' Lanny commanded.

Tremblingly they complied, the woman stumbling in her skirts as she stepped down.

The two men stood, utterly shaken, as Lanny frisked them, removing their wallets, gold watches, and a single-shot derringer pistol from the pocket of one. The woman had already removed her pearl necklace and she passed this to Lanny, saying, 'I've got nothing else of value.' Nonetheless, Lanny frisked her with a rough hand and concluded that she was speaking the truth.

Lanny addressed all three. 'Get walkin' down the road. Don't look back. If you do, you'll get a bullet.'

They were only too anxious to escape with their lives. Hastily they stumbled off, stepping round the body of the dead driver, taking care not to get blood on their shoes.

After pocketing his spoils Lanny jumped on to the coach and found the strongbox in a compartment beneath the driver's seat. It was chained to the floor, but he smashed the chain with two pistol shots. The box was heavy, but he hoisted it on to his shoulder and retraced his steps into the brush at the side of the trail. Further back, tethered in the trees, his horse awaited him. He mounted up, placing the box across the saddle in front of him. He kicked the animal into motion, having no wish to linger at this place. Let somebody else clear up the mess.

It was twenty miles to his hideout. He travelled in a triumphant mood. Gunning down men had given him an ecstasy akin to fornication.

★ ★ ★

Algernon Pike was six foot seven inches tall, several sizes larger than a Percheron stud horse. He had great brawny arms and legs, and hands like shovels.

He threw aside the hoe he had been using to drag weeds from the arid soil, and stooped through the low doorway of the shack. The place was unkempt and squalid. In the corner a woman sat, her big luminous eyes watching him. There was a duskiness to her skin, and she had long, shaggy hair that was a dull black. Her name was Stella.

On the rough mesquite-wood table was a plateful of fried corncake.

'Not damned corncake again!' he snarled.

'It's good food,' she said. 'You're lucky to have it.'

'Not for every meal! I'd rather eat the bark off trees!'

He was angry. He was like a great bear. He stepped forward, grabbed the plate in his paw of a hand, and threw it across the room.

For a moment the woman was fearful that he might come to her and beat her, like he had done before. But suddenly his mood shifted and his shoulders slumped. He swung around and went out through the doorway.

The shack, if such it could be called, had one room that was windowless. It was fashioned from timber and packed earth and was leaning against the hillside. Earth was constantly falling into the room from the roof, creating thick dust on the floor and on the crudely made table and two chairs. In the adjacent meadow, Pike had planted corn, and in a fenced-off corral a cow and a horse with bed-slat ribs grazed. The area was edged to the north by the great thicket of tangled mesquite, black chaparral and red oak.

Muttering curses to himself, Pike was picking up his hoe when he heard the thump of approaching hoofs. Glancing across, he saw a horseman emerging from the trees. He recognized him as Walking Hawk, the Kickapoo. He seemed to be swaying in his saddle. Pike frowned. He didn't trust Indians. A moment later a second rider appeared. Pike grunted with surprise. It was the marshal. The two reined in their horses on reaching Pike.

Stella had followed Pike out of the abode. Now she heard the exchange of words.

'You seen a stranger passin' through?' Blevins demanded breathlessly. 'He's the devil who gunned my brother down.'

Pike shook his shaggy head. 'Ain't seen nobody all mornin',' then he added, 'Is there a reward on offer?'

Blevins nodded. 'Sure there is, five hundred dollars. Dead or alive.'

'Well, if he does show up, I'll personally wring his neck.'

'His tracks pointed this way,' the marshal said. 'But I guess he bypassed this place. Can't be far ahead of us now.' With that he spurred his horse forward and, together with Walking Hawk, he galloped on and shortly disappeared into the thicket.

6

Brad Caulderfield had long since realized he was being pursued and he was growing tired of it. In consequence he took evasive action. On reaching a shallow stream he entered the water and set the buckskin along it. After a half-mile he left the stream on the same side as he'd entered it and circled back through the trees. He hoped that whatever tracks he'd left would confuse the men who followed him. Finding a suitable hiding place in a dense thicket of mesquite, he reined in and dismounted. He placed his hand across the muzzle of his animal to prevent it from communicating with any equine company in the vicinity. He waited, testing his snakebit leg and noting that most of the pain had gone. He had been damn lucky. Shortly he heard approaching horsemen and from his hiding place he glimpsed the riders — Blevins and Walking Hawk. He could feel his heart beating as he watched, scarcely daring to breathe. After a moment the tension eased in him. The riders disappeared from view and he heard them splashing across the stream, after which the thud of hoofbeats faded.

* * *

He lingered for a good half-hour; then, leading the horse, he made his way to the stream, crossed it, and shortly reached the edge of the meadowland. There was no sign of the marshal and his companion. Brad gazed across the open ground, seeing the primitive shack and the giant of a man working with a hoe in the cornfield.

He mounted the buckskin and heeled him forward. He was desperate with hunger and decided to chance his luck. The giant, hearing his approach, looked up, shading his eyes against the sun. As Brad rode to the edge of the cornfield he put aside his hoe, smiled and called out. 'Howdy, stranger. Welcome to my humble abode. I'm Algernon Pike. Pleased to meet you.'

'Have a couple o' riders passed this way?' Brad enquired.

Pike shook his head. 'Ain't seen nobody,' he lied. 'Anyway, come in and have a bite to eat. My woman'll fix you a fine plate of corncake.' Pike recalled that his rifle was leaning against the wall, just inside the shack. He also recalled that the marshal had said there was a reward on offer.

Brad did not trust the man. He was too affable to be true.

'Unsaddle your hoss,' Pike added. 'Put him in the corral.'

Brad hesitated, looking around to ensure that the marshal had not reappeared. 'I'll leave him saddled,' he said. 'I'll just hitch him here.' He fastened his reins to the pole fence of the corral.

Pike said, 'Your choice, mister. Come in, anyway.'

He led the way towards the abode, a few chickens scattering before him, and Brad followed, loosening his gun in its holster. Both men ducked their heads as they stepped inside. A stale, musty smell pervaded the place. In the shadows of the interior Brad glimpsed the woman coming to her feet. 'Howdy,' she murmured.

It was then that he saw the Winchester leaning against the wall, saw a sudden tightening in the muscles of Pike's back as he made a grab for the weapon. Brad had his Colt out instantly, ramming it into the giant's spine, pitching him forward. 'Touch that rifle an' I swear I'll kill you! Now get your hands up.'

Pike snarled out a curse, his mask of affability vanishing. He hesitated, then slowly raised his hairy arms, touching the roof with his hands.

Brad glanced into the frightened eyes of the woman. 'Get some rope,' he snapped out. She gave a nervous nod and darted out through the shack entrance. Brad wondered if he had taken a chance too many. She might never come back, or she might appear with another gun. Pike stood with his back turned, his great arms raised, cursing over and over.

'You ain't gonna get away with this. Marshal Blevins'll catch you an' string you up to the nearest tree. I know you killed his brother — and you'll damn well pay for it!'

To Brad's relief the woman returned holding a coiled rope. She looked at him enquiringly. For the first time he noticed her ripe mouth, her full breasts and body that were scarcely concealed by her tattered dress.

His attention returned to Pike. 'Lower your hands; put them behind your back,' he ordered. The giant grudgingly complied. Brad kept his gun levelled.

He nodded to the woman. 'Wind the rope around him . . . tight!'

To his surprise she said, 'It'll be a pleasure. It's all he's good for.' She set

about the task with obvious enthusi-
asm, binding the rope about him from
his chest to his waist and knotting it at
the end.

Brad prodded Pike over to the heap
of blankets in the corner of the room
and told him to lie down. Grunting
with displeasure, the giant slumped on
to what passed for a bed. While he was
helpless, Brad holstered his gun, took
hold of a blanket. He rolled it, drew it
around Pike's legs and tied it in a
strong knot. The blanket was filthy. As
he straightened up, fleas were jumping
on his hand.

From his supine position, Pike glared
at the woman and snarled, 'I'll kill you
for this!'

Brad had drawn his gun again and he
gestured with it threateningly. 'Not if I
plug you first!'

He glanced around and saw, on the
table, a plate piled high with corncake.

'Help yourself,' the woman said. 'He
won't be in no mood to eat it.'

It was stale but Brad had seldom

enjoyed a better meal. As he was finishing he tensed, hearing a horse whinnying from outside. He went to the doorway — and then relaxed. It was only the buckskin getting impatient at being tethered to the corral fence.

He turned back and again caught sight of the rifle leaning against the wall. He took hold of it. It was an old Fogerty rifle with a tube magazine in the butt. He removed the magazine and grunted with amusement. The magazine was empty.

Pike struggled in vain against his bonds. Giving up, he glared at Brad with smouldering eyes.

'Not loaded,' Brad commented.

'Damn right it ain't,' Pike growled. 'D'you figger I'd turn my back if that bitch had a loaded gun within reach?'

Brad reckoned he had spent sufficient time in conversation. He also reckoned that given time Pike would wriggle clear of the ropes. He walked out of the shack and threw the Fogerty as far as he could. He then went to his buckskin, untethered him and mounted up. He became aware that the woman had trailed after him.

'I'm comin' with you, mister,' she stated.

'You can't,' he said. 'The law's after me.'

'You can't leave me with *him*,' she snapped back. 'When he said he'd kill me, he sure meant it!'

A spare saddle and blanket were hanging from the corral fence. She lifted them off, hoisted them on to her shoulder, entered the corral and slapped them on to Pike's big sorrel mare. She was drawing the girth tight when Brad heeled the buckskin towards the brushland, the *brasada*. On reaching it he glanced back. She was following him, astride the sorrel, at a gallop.

He cursed. Life had a habit of punishing him with more complications than any man deserved.

7

Hanna Blevins, the marshal's sister, stepped briskly along the sidewalk of Buffalo Springs's main street, acknowledging the raised hat of the only passer-by. She was clutching her handbag, which contained her last month's earnings from the guest house. She intended to deposit the cash at the Western Bank, which was next to her brother's office. It was approaching noon and with the heat stoking up things were downright quiet.

Banks in the West were still scarce in number. In the past, folks had tended to carry their worldly wealth, hard-time tokens and stamp currencies around with them or hide them under their mattresses. This was risky. So when Henry Torgesen founded Torgesen's Western Bank in Buffalo Springs, the locals were delighted. Maybe it was a sodbuster bank, but it never issued wildcat money. It somehow signified the town's coming of age, and there was a mad stampede to deposit all available cash in its vault.

Hanna passed her brother's office, seeing Kenny Tolly standing in the doorway, his deputy's badge glinting in the sunlight. 'Good mornin', Miss Blevins,' he sang out, tipping his hat. 'The marshal's out catchin' the devil that killed your brother, so I'm keepin' law an' order today.'

Hanna greeted him with a curt nod, passed on by and entered through the open doorway of the bank. She was the only customer.

Henry Torgesen was adjusting the blinds at the windows. He was president of the bank, as well as being manager, teller, cashier, bookkeeper and general dogsbody. He added sophistication by wearing a boiled shirt, string tie, black coat and pinstripe trousers no matter how hot the day was. He hoped shortly to employ a helper.

'Good day, Miss Hanna,' he called out cheerfully as he took his place behind the counter.

Hanna, thankful for the coolness the bank offered after the heat outside, conducted her business and was refastening her empty handbag, when another customer walked in. He was a tall young man in a black hat with a silver band around it; he gave her a thin-lipped smile and went directly to the counter. He was carrying an empty gunny sack.

Torgesen, half-spectacles riding his nose, was busy behind his grille loading his coin box with silver dollars. He looked up and met the marble-hard, dark eyes of his customer. In that instant a pistol appeared in the man's hand.

'I want all the cash you've got,' he said matter of factly. 'And that includes everything in the vault.'

'But that's robbery,' Torgesen gasped in stunned disbelief, 'and robbery's a crime!'

The intruder thumbed back the hammer of his pistol with a loud click. 'Don't bullshit me. Unlock your counter an' let me in!'

Unbeknown to him, the man who threatened him was Lanny Caulderfield, Brad's wayward brother.

Torgesen glanced around, seeking support. All he saw was Hanna Blevins standing near the doorway, her eyes wide, her trembling hand raised to her mouth. She looked as if she was transfixed to the spot.

His face a deathly pallor, Torgesen looked back at Lanny, seeing how his expression was that of a maniac. Torgesen started to shake, but he moved along the counter and slid back the security bolt. As he turned towards the back-room vault, the pistol was jabbed in his back.

Using the combination, he opened the walk-in vault, and Lanny grunted appreciatively at the sight of shelf upon shelf of neatly bundled paper money, mostly greenbacks. He passed the grain sack to Torgesen and told him to hold it open.

Lanny rapidly scooped notes by the handful into the sack. As the last shelf was cleared the bell on the counter rang. From the back room they could not see who had entered the bank.

'I've come to draw some money,' a woman's voice called testily, '*if* you please.'

'Tell her you're sold out,' Lanny hissed.

Torgesen swallowed hard. His voice came with a noticable quiver. 'No cash available right now. Can you call back later?'

The lady muttered dissatisfaction, but left the bank.

Hoisting the sack over his shoulder, Lanny pushed aside Torgesen, moved around the counter and confronted Hanna Blevins, who appeared to be dumbstruck. He pointed his gun at her threateningly, but instead of pulling the trigger he reached out, snatched her handbag from her hand and slipped it into his sack.

She fainted, sinking to the floor.

But just then there was the sound of a drawer opening. Lanny turned to see Torgesen, behind the counter, aiming a derringer pistol, which he fired. But his trembling hand rendered the shot inaccurate and the bullet splintered the front window of the bank with a loud crack. Snarling like an animal, Lanny fired his own gun. The heavy bullet smashed into the bank president's chest and he was thrown back to disappear from view.

With Navy Colt raised and clutching the gunny sack, Lanny rushed out through the doorway, finding to his satisfaction that the sidewalk was deserted, though the sound of shots had caused some shouting at the end of the street. He did not delay, but unhitched his horse and vaulted into the saddle. He raked his spurs into the animal's flanks, turning it and catapulting it forward. Moments later he was making good his escape.

Meanwhile Hanna fluttered her eyelids as her senses returned. She glanced around, finding the bank silent. She climbed to her feet, conscious of the acrid smell of gunsmoke. She was angry with her brother the marshal. He should have prevented such an outrage. Then she remembered he was not in town. Well then, Kenny Tolly should have prevented it. She stumbled from the bank and went along the sidewalk to the marshal's office.

On entering she saw Kenny Tolly cowering under the desk.

'What are you doin' there?' she demanded.

He climbed to his feet, a sheepish look on his face. 'I heard shootin',' he explained. 'Is everythin' safe now?'

'You're employed to stop such outrages,' she shouted hysterically. 'That awful bandit stole my handbag!'

*　*　*

'We best stop here for a while,' Brad said. 'Give the hosses a breather.'

He and the black-haired woman had pulled up their mounts in a grassy break in the thicket. Wearily, they slid from their saddles and ground-tethered the lathered animals, which rested with their heads drooped. Presently they started to graze. They had travelled for hours, following game trails through the vast confusion of sunless copses that separated the open, bright-skied savannas, seeing mesquite trees heavy with beans, drinking from streams when they paused. The evening air was growing cool, the light fading. Brad was mightily thankful that there had been no sign of pursuit.

They sat down on the root of a tree.

'Call me Stella,' she said. 'What do I call you?'

He hesitated, then decided there was no harm in telling her his name, so he did.

He looked at her narrow face, saw the scars of suffering that it bore and the dark circles beneath her big eyes. But her lips still showed a voluptuousness that he guessed had pleased many a man.

She had snuggled up close to him. He could smell her sweat.

'Brad,' she murmured, 'I can't thank you enough for helpin' me escape from Algernon.'

'How come you got involved with him?' he asked.

'It was in Austin. I was a . . . saloon girl. He was one of my clients. He seemed a gentle giant. He told me I was the best girl he'd ever come across. He asked me to marry him. Lots of fellas had asked me to marry them an' hadn't meant it, but he seemed different. You mightn't believe it, but he could be very charmin' an' gentle when it suited him. He said he had a smallholding where the livin' was good. Well, I took him at his word an' ran away with him. I thought he'd protect me.'

'An' so you married him?'

She shook her head. 'From the start

he changed his mind, so we never got round to it, thank God, an' we ended up at that hovel. I never seen a man change like he did. After he'd had his way with me he became a monster. He beat me an' swore that if I tried to escape, he'd strangle me. I couldn't stand the thought of his great hands round my throat. I'm sure he's mad. I seen him strangle chickens, take a delight in it.' She groaned with abhorrence.

She rested her hand on his shoulder. She put her chin on her hand so that her lips were close to his ear. 'All I wanna do is find some man to protect me from Algernon. I'm so grateful to you. I can make you happy. I'll give you anythin' you want . . . anythin'!'

'Stella,' he said, 'you don't know me from Adam.'

'Brad, I know you killed a man — the marshal's brother.'

He was surprised. 'How come you know?'

'I heard the marshal tell Algernon,' she explained.

He made no comment.

Presently he said, 'I've already got a wife and a kid. An' that's where I'm headed now . . . home!' However a sudden surge of compassion came to him and he added, 'But I'll help you all I can.'

She emitted a sigh of relief. She gave him a light kiss on his cheek.

'You'll not regret it, Brad Caulderfield,' she whispered.

★ ★ ★

Shortly after they had left Algernon Pike's meagre property, Walking Hawk fell off his horse. Marshal Blevins cursed him, regretting that he had put his faith in the tracking skills of the Indian. He dismounted, picked up the man's canteen and uncorked it, sniffing the pungent odour of rot-gut whiskey. 'Always knew you couldn't take your drink,' he commented. Walking Hawk sat where he had fallen, gazing at his superior with ashamed, bloodshot eyes.

Blevins cursed him and told him to stand up and get back on his horse. The Indian mumbled something and experienced some difficulty in climbing back into his saddle.

Later, despite probing deep into tangled thicket, they had failed to pick up any recognizable tracks. The Indian's eyes had become bleary and the marshal had concluded that before long they would be lost. Once more cursing his wretched luck, knowing that he would have his sister Hanna's scornful tongue-lashing to contend with, he decided to turn back. When Walking Hawk again fell from his horse and started singing what sounded like his death-song, Blevins left him. The Indian would have to make his own way home when he sobered up.

It was almost dark when he eventually reached Pike's shack. A faint light glowed from within and as he approached the giant figure of Pike stepped out, holding a lantern, and looking as tetchy as a teased snake. He recognized the marshal who rode up and slid from the back of his tuckered-out horse.

'You catch that sonofabitch?' Pike demanded.

Blevins cursed, shaking his head. 'He gave us the slip, I guess. He's got the luck o' the devil. I've ridden the hocks off my damn hoss trying to find him!'

'Well, I mean to track him down,' the giant homesteader said, anger spiking his voice. 'He's stolen my hoss an' kidnapped my woman. He left me trussed up like a turkey an' it was all I could do to wriggle free. I'll find him and I'll strangle the bastard!'

'Trouble is,' Blevins said, 'we don't know who he is an' where he's headed.'

'Well, my woman's got kin in Austin. She'll most likely go there. First thing I'll do is go to town and get myself a hoss.'

Blevins smoothed his moustache thoughtfully. 'If she was kidnapped she'll go where the sonofabitch takes her, which could be anywhere.'

Pike shuffled his feet awkwardly, then he made an admission. 'I guess she didn't offer much resistance when he took her. She'll probably head where she wants.'

Blevins looked at the corral, saw that its sole occupant was a cow. 'If you're gonna go to town afoot, you sure have a lengthy walk. I can't offer to take you on my hoss. She'd collapse under the weight. She's worn out already.'

'Come mornin',' Pike said, 'I'll walk. I've got long legs.'

Blevins changed the subject. 'Have you got somethin' to eat? I'm right starvin'.'

Pike nodded. 'I just killed a chicken. You can have a bit o' that.'

8

In the days after Stella's escape from Algernon Pike Brad had succumbed to her pleas and escorted her to Austin. At first he imagined that he would search in Austin for his brother, but subsequently he concluded that it would be too risky; he might be recognized. During the intervening days they had lived off the game he shot and cooked over campfires — mainly squirrel. They had travelled through the *brasada*, bathing in streams; the life they encountered included turkey gobblers, *javelinas*, and the occasional wild bull. At night, as they snuggled in the sougan, they were serenaded by the hooting of owls and the yip-yap of vixens.

He had unfastened the bandage that Doc Murphy had placed around his leg and was pleased to see that the swelling had gone down and the puncture was scarcely discernible.

When they left the *brasada* they travelled across swaths of grassland and here they came upon human habitation. For sustenance and respite, they stopped at an isolated community where folk were German settlers. He purchased a coat and dress for her, pants for himself. He was ever watchful that somebody might recognize him as a wanted killer, but he consoled himself with the hope that distance and delay in communication would render that unlikely, at least until they reached Austin, where the law and telegraph prevailed.

Stella had proved strange company. Her resentment, her sulkiness, had fluctuated with moods of profound endearment as the miles fell behind them. At times she had shown him great affection, choosing the nights, spent in the open, to snuggle up to him, kissing, caressing him, whispering enticement. She could not rouse him. His only response had been to hold her silently in his arms, to create some warmth against the chill. Thoughts of Mary-Ellen and his love for her remained in his mind. However he felt obliged to keep his word and deliver Stella to Austin.

She could not understand him. She had never encountered a man so unresponsive to her, and yet she cherished his nearness. She felt the need for his presence not only to guide her through the wild country, but because he created feelings in her that she had never experienced before.

When they reached a hill overlooking Austin, Brad reined in. The sprawling city lay before them. Carved out of the wilderness, now boasting a railroad, it was backed by green rolling hills that had once been the domain of marauding Comanches.

'This is as far as I'm goin',' he said, turning to her. They had dismounted and stood facing each other. 'This is where you wanted to come. I kept my word. Maybe you'll be safe in Austin. I wouldn't be.'

He reached out his hand and said, 'Good luck, Stella.'

She accepted his handshake, but then she leaned across, grasped his arm and pulled him towards her. She kissed his lips. Now that the moment had come, she knew she would miss him.

'Come into town for a while,' she said. 'Nobody'll recognize you here.'

He shook his head. 'I been away far too long. I gotta get back home now.' In his mind was the vague hope that Lanny might have returned to the homestead, and that somehow the situation with Mulvaney would be resolved.

'Where's home?' Stella asked, trying to hide her eagerness for an answer.

He gave her a wry smile.

'A long way off,' was all he said, then he turned to his buckskin, mounted, and rode off. When he glanced back, she was gone.

★   ★   ★

Angry resentment burned in Stella. What right had he to reject her love?

In town, she stabled her horse in a livery and made her way through familiar alleyways to the Lucky Strike saloon in Pecan Street. The place was practically empty, but a pianist was tinkling on the tin piano. Bald-headed Sam Makepeace, the proprietor, was behind the bar polishing glasses when he saw her.

His face lit up and he said, 'Why honey, I sure am glad to see you. Have a whiskey. Where the hell have you been?'

'On vacation,' she said. 'I'd like my room back again, Sam.'

He checked his board and reached down a key which he slid across the bar to her. 'It's all yours. Number 14. It'll be a treat to have you here once more.'

She tossed back her drink in one gulp. Damn Brad Caulderfield, she thought. She would teach him a lesson.

Once in her upstairs room she washed, then she went down to the street and walked briskly to the town marshal's office. She was furious with Brad. She'd offered him everything and he had spurned her. But she had his name and that would give the law something to work on.

However she was frustrated to find the office closed and locked up. On the door was a sign saying 'Back Thursday afternoon'. She snorted with displeasure, today being Tuesday. She was turning to retrace her steps when the frontage of the telegraph office caught her eye. Her spirits lifted. She would send a telegram to Marshal Blevins in Buffalo Springs.

Over the next two nights she made a good profit from her clients, enough in fact to make a purchase that she had set her mind on. She visited Hoffman's general store down the street from the saloon, which stocked everything from farm tools to Toneco Stomach Bitters. Having studied the firearms on display, she purchased a short-barrelled derringer pistol with a large bore, and some bullets to go with it. It fitted snugly in her pocket. If Algernon found her she would be ready for him. But thoughts of Algernon did not dominate her thoughts. Thoughts of Brad Caulderfield did.

Remorse struck her. She was utterly mixed up. The resentment she felt against Brad had melted away. She felt herself yearning for him. She bitterly regretted sending the telegram to Marshal Blevins. She had acted on the spur of the moment. She had felt incensed, but now those emotions had gone and she realized that, for the first time in her life, she had been in love.

★ ★ ★

In the graveyard behind the church the funeral attracted a crowd, and it was a far bigger occasion than Seth Blevins had anticipated, for it entailed the burying of his brother Frank as well as Henry Torgesen. When the marshal had returned to Buffalo Springs he had been horrified to learn of the bank robbery and the murder of its much respected owner. It had been generally expressed in the town that Blevins should have concentrated on maintaining order locally instead of wandering off in pursuit of the man who had killed his brother. In addition Hanna had lambasted him to such an extent that it could have been no worse had he committed the bank robbery himself.

'That bandit could've killed me,' she raged, 'an' then what would you have done?'

'Celebrated,' he had muttered under his breath.

The minister proclaimed that the ways of the Lord were mysterious, and that the Lord giveth and the Lord taketh away. At that moment a strong gust of wind came, blowing several hats off heads, and there was a mad rush to recover them. Once everybody was settled they all sang a hymn, after which the earth was spaded in on the coffins. Seth Blevins thought: Two men, a banker and a drunkard, who in life had probably never said a word to each other, and now they were lying side by side for eternity, sharing a common link of being victims of murder.

Afterwards, the mourners drifted home, and Blevins made his way to his office. The boy from the telegraph office was waiting outside and he handed over a telegram. Blevins tipped the boy, went in and put on his spectacles. A moment later he was reading the message.

Name of man you want for murder of your brother is Brad Caulderfield.

I got this name at great risk and expect to be rewarded.

Contact me at Lucky Strike Saloon Austin.

Signed: Stella Goodnight

Blevin's blood pressure had risen. If the message was genuine, a valuable piece of the jigsaw had fallen into place and he could get hand bills circulated. WANTED *dead or alive*.

The saloon was packed when Stella returned from a late-night supper at the restaurant next door. There were loud-mouthed crowds lining the bar, three poker tables were in operation, foaming schooners of beer were clinking, and the pianist was accompanied by a man playing the fiddle. In addition, five ruby-lipped girls were plying their charms on customers, trying to entice them to the upstairs rooms. The whole place reeked of the rough perfume of cigars, spittoons of tobacco juice, stale beer and sweat.

The proprietor, Sam Makepeace, caught Stella's eye and sauntered over to her, meeting her at the far end of the bar. He had to speak in a loud voice to make himself heard above the din.

'Hi honey. Fella came in asking specifically for you. I told him you'd be back soon and he said he'd wait upstairs.'

Stella nodded. It was not unusual for

her to be requested by name. She was turning towards the stairs when Make-peace added, 'He was a mighty big fella.'

Her heart missed a beat. For a moment she was in a trance. In her estimation there was only one 'big fella' in her world.

'Say, you all right, honey?' Make-peace enquired.

She steeled herself. 'Sure I am. I'll go up now.'

She was halfway up the staircase when she paused, took the derringer from her pocket and double-checked that it was loaded. There was a slight tremor in her hands. Holding the pistol within the folds of her skirt, she continued up on to the landing and gazed down the lamplit hallway. There was nobody there. On tentative feet, she tiptoed along the carpeted floor until she reached her room: number 14 with her name beneath. She knew that Algernon was on the other side of the door because she smelt him.

Furthermore, she could see a strip of light beneath the door.

Gathering her courage, she turned the handle and thrust the door open. He was standing by the window, gazing into the street outside — but he twisted immediately, his face contorted with malice. She raised the derringer, pulled the trigger. He threw himself to the side as the gun went off and the bullet, instead of ploughing into his chest as she'd intended, clipped his right earlobe.

Like a catamount, he sprang for her. He grabbed her wrist, twisted it, forcing her to drop the pistol. He lifted her off her feet as if she was a rag doll. His face, close to hers, was filled with maniacal hatred, his lips sprayed spittle. Then, with massive force, he hurled her on to the bed. He rammed his knee into her ribcage, making her cry out with pain; he knelt on her with all his great weight. 'You bitch,' he snarled, 'you ran away with your fancy man, but he won't do you no good now. I'll kill him just the same as I gonna kill you!' She tried to scream but the pressure of him had expelled every last breath from her lungs.

Now his huge hands found her throat, increasing an iron grip on her windpipe. Teeth bared, his stare merciless on her bulging, terrified eyes, he did not relax his hold until she lay still. At that moment a sharp rap on the door sounded.

'Are you OK, Stella?' came the concerned voice of Sam Makepeace.

Pike cursed to himself. He stood up, ready to face Makepeace if he barged in. But he did not, and in a firm voice Pike called out. 'Sure, she's OK. A man don't expect to be interrupted when he's paid good money.'

He heard Makepeace say, 'Just wondered.' Then his receding footsteps sounded.

Pike's breathing steadied. His face was glistening with sweat. He could hear the riotous babble from downstairs in the saloon. It seemed a world away.

He forced himself to relax. He was annoyed that he had lost the lobe of his ear. Glancing round, he noticed a paper on the table. It was a telegram. He picked it up, read it.

Reference your telegram. when Brad Caulderfield is arrested or his body brought in and guilt is confirmed, I will recommend that you receive a reward. Signed: Seth Blevins, Marshal Buffalo Springs.

Pike uttered a grunt of understanding. He repeated the name: 'Brad Caulderfield', and stuffed the telegram into his pocket. He took one final look at the body, then he left the room, walked along the hallway and down the stairs.

Sam Makepeace saw him and said, 'Mister, you got blood down the side of your face.'

Pike forced himself to laugh. 'It's my ear,' he said huskily. 'That Stella . . . she's got sharp teeth!'

Makepeace smiled knowingly. As Pike left the saloon the saloon proprietor ran up the stairs to the upper floor. He was not happy about Stella.

Pike stepped out on to the sidewalk. He was glad of the cool night air on his face. He walked to the livery in long strides. He quickly got his horse from its stall, saddled it, paid the hostler and mounted up. Within five minutes he had quit Austin and was riding away beneath the stars. The name Caulderfield was familiar to him. He could recall delivering corn-feed to their place at Chippers Creek. Now the name of *Brad* Caulderfield was branded into his mind — the focus of his satanic hatred.

9

Brad returned to the homestead on Chippers Creek. He had pressed the buckskin hard, driven by a feeling that time was running out and the date for eviction was growing ever closer. He still harboured the hope that Lanny might have preceded him, but he knew it was highly unlikely and the weight of failure dragged at him like a millstone.

He found his father sitting in a rocking chair on the veranda, a Winchester slanted across his lap. His tired face brightened when he recognized his son, his eyes questioning.

After they had greeted each other, Brad got straight to the point.

'I'm sorry, Pa. I didn't find him.'

The old man sighed, as if he had suspected all along that this would be the case.

'Why the gun?' Brad asked.

'I keep it ready in case Lanny comes back.'

'You mean you'd . . . gun him down?'

'He ain't no good. He's a disgrace to the family. He don't deserve nothin' better'n a bullet.'

Brad frowned.

The old man said, 'Sheriff Blevins from Buffalo Springs has been sniffin' round here, askin' after you. Twice he's been over. I told him you hadn't been here for months and I wasn't expectin' you back. I don't trust anybody wearin' a badge. You done somethin' wrong, Brad?'

At that moment Mary-Ellen, who had been cooking supper, stepped out from the house, and emitted a cry of delight. Immediately she was in Brad's arms, murmuring, 'Oh honey, I'm so glad you're home. Thank God.'

He hugged on to her, unable to help tears of joy moistening his eyes. He kissed her, knowing that he could never care for any other woman. 'How's babe?' he whispered.

'She'll be the better for havin' you back.'

Brad laughed happily.

Over supper they listened as he told how he had looked for Lanny, searching high and low. Then he got around to the shooting of the marshal's brother and subsequent troubles, including the snakebite. He showed them what remained of the scar.

They listened in stunned silence.

It was past ten o'clock when Brad and Mary-Ellen returned to their own cabin. Annie Carter, Dan's wife, had long since put baby Betsy in her cot. Annie was thrilled that Brad had come home and hugged him to her large, billowy bosom, after which Brad gazed at his sleeping daughter and a surge of pride brought a smile to his face. But at the back of his mind, he was haunted by events of the past. Once in bed, he took Mary-Ellen in his arms and again went over what had happened to him. When he had finished she wept and it was a long time before either of them could sleep.

Next morning they went up to the main cabin and found William Caulder-field in a low mood.

'Brad, I dunno what we're gonna do. Time's getting' short now, an' I'm sure Mulvaney won't hesitate when it comes to evictin' us.'

'Mebbe I should ride over an' see him,' Brad suggested. 'Who knows? We might be able to reach some compromise.'

His father nodded and said, 'I guess anythin's worth a try, but I don't hold out much hope.'

An hour later, Brad left on the buckskin. Like the old man, he knew that Mulvaney wasn't the type to go back on his ultimatum, but their options were running out — just like time.

* * *

Algernon Pike had spied on the homestead for two days, keeping himself hidden in a thicket of scrub oak to the west, his new Springfield fast-loader, traded from an army sergeant, at the ready. He had seen Brad Caulderfield moving about the smallholding, and his pulse had quickened. He could have shot at him, maybe downed him, but he didn't favour such action. At that range he might have missed anyway. What he preferred was to bide his time, to catch Brad at a moment convenient to himself, when he couldn't fail. He wanted Brad to die slowly so he knew that Algernon Pike was getting his revenge. He would wound him first with a bullet, but not fatally, and then, when he was ready, he would get his hands around his throat and choke him to death.

He was out of his bedroll and fully alert by the time he spotted Brad leaving the homestead. He snarled softly to himself, like a cougar sensing its prey. Within a minute his quarry would be in the sights of the Springfield.

Over the past weeks Brad had got into the habit of being alert. He knew he was hated by at least three men, all of whom wanted him dead. But he wasn't ready to die yet. Mary-Ellen and the babe had given him everything to live for, not to mention his father, and within a few short weeks they could all be dispossessed of everything they had worked for. He knew that Mulvaney wouldn't hesitate to send in his cowboys to destroy their homesteads and their entire livelihood when he judged the time to be ripe. He was not a patient man.

Pike's sorrel mare was tethered well back in the trees and out of view — but the sixth-sense possessed by equines warned her of the approaching buckskin. Suddenly she unleashed an ear-splitting whinny.

Alarmed, Brad reined back with such abruptness that the buckskin reared up, throwing him from the saddle. It was at that precise moment that Pike pressed the trigger — but it was the buckskin, risen on hind legs, that caught the bullet in the chest. He screamed in agony, then plunged down and rolled over on to his side; his hoofs flailed for an instant and then grew still, his stiffened legs extended.

Brad had fallen heavily, furious at being outwitted. He realized that he was lying on open prairie and at any second the marksman concealed in the thicket might unleash a second shot. He was right. As, crablike, he propelled himself with his hands and toes towards his fallen horse, a bullet passed so close to his ear that he felt its deadly breath. He made it to the animal, sprawled down against the beast's belly, keeping his head low. His heart was pounding. The cover was inadequate, but there was no other. He felt a further bullet thud into the buckskin's back. He cursed. A burst of fury burned through his body like an outpouring of molten lava. What right had this bastard to kill a faithful animal that, even in death, still served him?

He unholstered his Colt, eased back the hammer.

He was aware of the sun, burning into the back of his neck. Sweat was beading out on his body. Myriads of bluebottle flies swarmed about the carcass of the horse, some of them trying to settle on Brad, setting up an incessant buzz. He wondered how long he could stay in his present position. He risked a glance above his cover and saw the thicket of oak. Nothing moved there. He ducked down again, pondering on when his attacker would play another card. He wondered who he was: Marshal Blevins, Algernon Pike, or even his brother Lanny? All were deadly in their hate for him. Or perhaps it was some unknown bounty hunter out to make a quick buck.

At that moment a movement caught his eye. Glancing up, he saw three buzzards cruising the heavens. They glided in big, looping circles. He shuddered.

What should he do? To leave his

present cover could be tantamount to suicide. Maybe he should wait through the remaining hours of the day and try to escape under the cloak of darkness. On the other hand, his attacker might think him dead and quit his own hiding place to come and investigate. He could not afford for the man to creep up on him, and yet to keep surveillance entailed lifting his head and risking having it blown off.

As a test he hoisted his hat above his cover. The immediate outcome was that a bullet whined its way perilously close, drawing a curse from his lips. There was no doubt about it. He was well and truly pinned down.

He waited out the torrid afternoon hours, driven nigh crazy by the flies. The pungent stench that emanated from the carcass made breathing nauseating and seemed to envelope his body and clothing. Cramp gripped his legs, but any relieving movement would have exposed him.

At long, long last the sun settled into

its westward drift, painting the grass-lands a fiery red and diminishing the day's stifling heat. He prayed that an impenetrable darkness would come soon and he determined to make his move before the moon and stars took hold. He formed a plan, driven by hatred for the sonofabitch who had placed him in this horrendous predica-ment and killed his horse. He felt that his enemy might suspect that, if he did attempt an escape, he would head back towards the homestead. He therefore decided to head in the opposite direction and after a while to circle around and approach the thicket, and his enemy, from the rear. He would kill him without compunction. All he needed was inky darkness and a generous slice of good fortune.

It took another hour for sufficient darkness to descend. He stretched his limbs, easing the kinks from his bones as best he could. Then, taking a deep breath, he wormed his way clear of the carcass, hugging the ground, his spine tingling at the prospect of a sudden thwack of lead, but none came. Five minutes later he rose to his feet and set off at a brisk walk, thankful for the Stygian gloom and the fresh coolness of the air. Presently he started to run.

When he was a good mile away from spot where he had been bushwhacked, he cut around to his left and after some ten minutes he reached the back of the shadowy thicket. He forced himself to pause, allowing his breathing to steady and cease its rasp. When he was satisfied he checked his Colt and crept forward, moving with infinite care to avoid disturbing the tangled under-growth. Even so, he was unable to prevent thorns snatching at his clothing and scratching his hands.

He recalled that his assailant's horse had been hidden somewhere in the thicket. At any moment, if it was still here, the animal might betray his presence. On the other hand, if it had gone, it would be an indication that his assailant had also departed.

He was easing into motion once more when he heard the sound of grass, gripped by equine teeth, being pulled. It emanated from not far to his left. He paused, his mind full of uncertainty — and then came a nervous snort. It was obvious that the animal was close-hobbled, and he didn't know whether its master was within earshot. He took a chance, drifted in the direction of the horse and found the small clearing where it stood. Before it could make further utterance he had reached it, was smoothing its extended nostrils and whispering comforting murmurings. He felt the nervous quivering in the horse lessen.

He lingered for five minutes, ensuring that the animal remained calm, at the same time allowing his own agitation to abate. He took stock. Through the tangle of branches over his head he could see the sliver of the moon. He reckoned that he was halfway through the thicket and ahead of him must be the point from which his assailant had fired at him. Was he still there?

With the utmost caution he probed his way forward, wincing at the cruel stabbing of thorns. Then, more suddenly than he had anticipated, the undergrowth thinned before him and he could see across the open, sloping ground. There, in the moonlight, lay the shadowy hulk of the dead buckskin. He saw movement about it and he realized that the buzzards were ripping out the entrails. And then he swallowed hard as he glimpsed further movement. From across to his left a huge wraithlike figure was ascending the incline. Brad tightened his grip on his gun, a name hammering at his mind: Algernon Pike!

The giant had obviously gone down to investigate whether his quarry still survived, and to administer the final killing if so. But he had been thwarted, and in his frustration he was returning to his horse. Brad waited, holding his breath, cursing as the thumping of his heart increased, and he was reminded of another such moment in his past.

But the infuriating fact was that Pike was going to enter the thicket at a spot some distance to Brad's left. He would disappear into the brush before he could get a shot at him.

10

Within the thicket pitch darkness prevailed, the slim moon's light blocked out by tangled branches. Brad crouched down, pondering what to do. Pike had disappeared into the thicket some ten yards to the left, and now he made no attempt to conceal his presence as he blundered through the undergrowth. This indicated that he was unaware he had company. It seemed he was heading for the clearing in which his mare was hobbled.

Brad rose to his feet and followed up on the other man's floundering progress, hearing his curses as thorns punished him. Suddenly Brad caught his toe on a tree root and fell, creating a loud rustling of foliage. He was aware that Pike had stopped moving, no doubt alarmed by the sound. He heard the metallic click of a pistol being cocked.

Suddenly that gun blasted off, creating a spurt of orange flame as lead splintered the bark of a close-in tree, making Brad duck. At that moment the mare unleashed its panicking whinny. Brad raised his gun and fired at the point from which Pike's shot had shown. As the ringing in his ears subsided, the only sound was the whisper of the night breeze in the branches. Then the horse whinnied again with increased urgency.

Another shot roared out and Brad felt the searing burn of lead across the muscle of his left arm. In a spasm of pain and fury he stood up and fired a shot at the point from which the latest spurt of flame had erupted. There was an immediate response — a long groan followed by the sound of a heavy body falling into the undergrowth.

Gun cocked and raised, Brad stepped forward. A moment later, he almost stumbled over Pike's belly-up body. He stooped down, pressing the muzzle of his weapon to the man's head, but suddenly Pike jerked his brawny arm upward, brushing Brad aside as he pulled his trigger. The shot whined off into the darkness.

Pike rose up, like a monster emerging from the deep, his great hands encircling Brad's throat. Brad was forced back, the giant's weight crushing him. He felt the tightening grip on his windpipe, tried in vain to draw in breath. His senses were becoming blurred, and in the background the horse was neighing frantically. He could feel the blood oozing out from his left arm. He felt like a sponge being squeezed.

He realized that his outflung right hand still gripped his pistol, his finger curled around the trigger. Somehow he found the strength to cock the weapon with his thumb and press the muzzle into Pike's side. The detonation came with a deafening roar, causing a convulsion in the man's immense body, and a slackening of his grip around Brad's throat.

After that Brad blacked out.

It was still dark when he blinked his way to consciousness.

Pike's body lay on top of him, making breathing difficult. He tried to heave it off, but his hands were so slippery with blood that it took three attempts before he was able to squirm free. He satisfied himself that Pike was dead, then sat for a while, taking in the fact that he himself had somehow survived this horrific ordeal. He rubbed his throat. It felt bruised and swallowing was painful.

Presently he clambered unsteadily to his feet and found his way to the clearing where the mare waited patiently. She stood with nostrils twitching, ears set forward. He smoothed her withers with a gentle touch of his hand, then he fumbled with the hobbles and unshackled them. The beast had been left saddled for what must have been hours. Pike had needed a big mount to carry his bulk. Now, Brad grasped the reins and led her out of the thicket. He slipped his foot into the stirrup and hauled himself on to her back. He touched his heels to her flanks and soon was galloping across the prairie, homeward bound. Tomorrow he would bring a wagon out and convey Pike's corpse to a suitable place for dumping.

★　★　★

Lanny delighted in pulling away the rock that covered his cache of loot. He loved to finger the banknotes. The fact that he was now a rich man filled him with dreams of an orgiastic future. He reckoned he would go north to Wyoming or Montana, where he was unknown and where, from all reports, there were rich pickings to be had. He was still sure that there was nothing to associate him with the two heists and the killings that he had carried out. In the stagecoach robbery he had worn a bandanna over his face, and in the bank robbery the only people to see his face had been the now-dead bank manager and that silly old woman, who no doubt had a flea-bitten memory.

But before he travelled north he had two tasks to complete: two tasks before which his other successes paled to insignificance.

The memory of years of resentment and jealousy had festered in his mind. He had hated his father for his overbearing ways, and for always pandering to Brad because he was dumb enough to work his guts out on the smallholding. He had despised Brad because he had got himself a fancy wife who was too good to be true, whereas the best *he'd* managed was a flippity little rancher's daughter who'd nearly died of fright when he'd shown some passion.

Brad had always been contemptuous of his free-spirited nature and in those last months, had considered it beneath his dignity even to utter a word to him. When he had walked out on his father and brother, Lanny had made a promise: *One day soon, I'll kill you both*! And now he smiled smugly and prided himself in the belief that he was a man of his word.

He also promised himself an indulgence to satisfy his craving for female comfort. He had been denied a woman for too long.

He spent a whole evening, crouched in his hideout, cleaning his weapons and making plans.

★ ★ ★

Mary-Ellen had carefully bathed and bandaged the wound in Brad's arm. He had been lucky, for the bullet had done nothing more than burn a groove across the muscle, but it had bled considerably. She was horrified when she learned how close she had come to losing her husband. His father was similarly sympathetic and shocked.

On the morning following the killing of Pike, Brad and the Negro Dan Carter took out a wagon to collect the corpse. Getting it out of the thicket was backbreaking work, and they used a rope to raise it up on to the wagon. Decomposition had already set in, bringing a smell so vile that they lifted their bandannas over their noses, and the flies swarmed all around.

Having loaded the body, Brad walked down to where the remains of the buckskin lay. Buzzards flapped skywards as he approached. Waving aside more flies, he saw how the scavengers had stripped away the flesh and eyes of the animal. What was left was scarcely more than a skeleton. He unstrapped his saddle, dragged it clear of the horse and put it on the wagon. He cursed Pike for what he had done and felt no remorse as he rejoined Dan Carter on the seat.

They drove to a spot on the prairie well away from the homestead and sweated under the scorching sun as they dug a large hole. Without ceremony they dropped the body into it and spaded in the earth, leaving only a bare, stamped-down patch to indicate where the grave was — a patch that would soon be reclaimed by nature. Then they returned to the homestead.

That afternoon he worked on the roof of the new barn, nailing in slats. He wondered whether he was wasting his time, and whether, within a few short weeks, the whole spread would be reclaimed by Mulvaney. Thinking of the rancher, he decided to make another attempt at trying to reach a compromise.

Accordingly, the next morning he saddled Pike's sorrel mare. He smoothed her mane and neck, remembering how she had saved his life by carrying warning of danger to him. He bade his wife and father farewell and headed out. He passed the thicket with some trepidation, his spine twitching as he subconsciously feared that Pike's ghost might have returned to exact revenge. But he rode on, the only movements, apart from his own, coming from the birds in the sky, the crickets in the grass and a scurry of distant pronghorns.

As he drew closer to the Bar-B ranch he encountered scattered herds of red-and-white Hereford cattle. He reached the ranch house at about noon and reined up in the yard fronting it. In a corral a cowboy was breaking in a pony and more cowboys were leaning on the surrounding fence, cheering him on. Some of them he knew from visits to Summerton and he exchanged waves. He dismounted, fastened his mare to the hitching rail and climbed the steps to the main door. He rang the handbell.

Consuelo, Mulvaney's young Mexican wife, appeared from the shadowed interior, wiping her hands on her apron. She looked scarcely old enough to have a seventeen-year-old daughter.

'*Señor*?' she enquired.

'Is the major at home?' he asked.

'*Sí*. Who shall I say eet is?'

'Brad Caulderfield.'

Her expression hardened but she nodded. 'Come in. I will fetch heem.'

She turned and disappeared through a doorway.

Removing his Stetson, he stepped into the main room of the ranch house. It was cool after the blazing sun.

His gaze took in cushioned, high-backed sofas and a handsome painting of Custer's Last Battle on the wall. He stood on the carpeted floor, listening to the loud tick of the fine grandfather clock which stood in the corner. He was fascinated by the constant swing of the pendulum.

'You got a cheek!' Major Mulvaney's voice came like a whiplash as he stepped into the room. 'I never figgered a Caulderfield would darken my doorway ever again.' His bearded face was flushed with anger. He was holding a plaited quirt which he slapped against his thigh.

Brad forced himself to keep calm. 'Major Mulvaney, I've searched high an' low for my brother an' found no trace of him. My father's worried sick about bein' evicted. He's a crippled ol' man, an' I just don't know what he'll do if you force him outa the homestead. It'll most likely kill him. He's lived there for thirty years, fought off Injuns an' rustlers.'

'That's not my concern,' Mulvaney bristled. 'After what a Caulderfield did to my daughter, you can all go to hell so far as I care. I want you off my land in a month's time unless you deliver your brother, or his dead body, to me before that. I can't make it damned clearer!'

Brad swallowed hard and tried a different approach. 'Surely there can be some compromise? We want Lanny brought to account same as you. Both Pa an' me are downright disgusted at what Lanny did, just as much as you are.'

'Not as much as me.' Mulvaney stepped to the doorway leading to the kitchen and yelled: 'Lilith! Come here.'

For a moment it seemed there would be no response, but then the girl shuffled in. She was wearing an apron and held a knife. She had most likely been peeling potatoes.

'Show him, gal,' her father demanded loudly.

She hesitated, then drew back her apron.

Brad gasped at the sight of her swollen belly.

'It's Lanny Caulderfield's bastard child,' Mulvaney said. 'Now you know why you can never feel as bad as I do. I've long concluded that all Caulderfields are tarred with the same damn brush. Now kindly leave my house an' don't come back.' He raised the quirt.

The rancher was a merciless bully; nothing would change that. Brad was speechless. After a moment he gave a nod to Mulvaney and the girl, rammed on his hat and stamped out. There was nothing to be gained here.

11

Two afternoons later Lanny rode into Buffalo Springs, confident that nobody would in any way connect him with recent events. He smiled to himself as he passed the Western Bank, the windows boarded up and a sign *Closed Until Further Notice* on the door. Some of the local traders were going to be downright sore at losing their money.

The town was moderately busy. He held his head high, tipping his hat to the ladies. Having lodged his horse at the livery, he purchased himself a new set of clothing, then he visited Jack's Tonsorial Parlour, had a hot bath followed by a haircut and shave. Now he felt ready to enjoy himself. First, he went to a restaurant and had a slap-up meal of pork, potatoes, beans and corn. Next, he made his way to the Lucky

Ace, the biggest of the local thirst parlours, where he set himself up with a bottle of whiskey and retired to a table.

The place was already bustling with its evening trade, a crowd of miners having hit town, looking for some gaiety. A plumpish woman in a short skirt and striped stockings was attempting to sing *Cotton-Eyed Joe* accompanied by a man on a squeeze-box, and there were several card tables on the go.

Before long a surprisingly fresh-faced girl in a low cut dress appeared at his shoulder. 'Buy a drink for a gal, mister?' she asked. He eyed her up and down. She had impudent blue eyes and lips that were a shocking pink. He liked the curves of her body. She would look good when he ripped her clothes off. He nodded and waved to a waiter to set her up. She sat down beside him, and as she sipped her whiskey she placed her free hand on his thigh. He felt an erection stirring. She sensed it, laughed and said, 'If you wanna pop your cork, cowboy, we'll go upstairs. Only ten dollars.' Again he nodded.

Carrying a half-empty bottle of liquor, he followed her across the room and up the staircase, passing a sign which said: *Satisfaction Guaranteed, Or Money Refunded*.

Later, when he came downstairs he knew that he had been rough with the girl, literally a lawful rape, but she hadn't cried out. Now he felt half satiated. It was getting late and he didn't fancy the ride back to his hideout, so he asked a bartender which was the best boarding house in town. 'Three blocks down on the left, a place called the Golden Rest,' the man advised. 'Don't go to the Blevins place. They charge the earth.'

Lanny nodded his thanks and went as directed, but there was a sign saying FULL UP hanging in the window. There was another boarding house further along and, on enquiring, he was told there was no space left there either. 'But try the Blevins place; it's next to the livery.' He had been warned against it, but he was not short of money.

He was welcomed by the marshal, Seth Blevins, though Lanny didn't know him. Yes, they had a room if he didn't mind sharing with two others. 'Room One, top o' the stairs. Payment up front.'

'That's OK,' Lanny said. 'Have you any whiskey?'

Blevins shook his head, noting the strong taint on the stranger's breath. 'We don't sell liquor.'

Blevins wrote out a bill which Lanny paid. It was mighty high, but he did not complain.

'Stranger in Buffalo Springs?' Blevins asked, always inquisitive about faces he did not know.

'Just passin' through,' Lanny responded, then he added, 'Can you fix me a supper?'

'Well, my sister usually deals with that side o' business, but she's out at a church meeting right now. I've gotta go out soon myself, but I guess I can do you some beef an' bread if that'll suit you.'

Lanny accepted the offer and was

shown into the dining room which was furnished with tables and chairs. There were two other men seated there, playing cribbage. He nodded to them but they were too engrossed with their game to pay him any attention.

He sat down at a table and shortly Blevins brought in a huge hunk of bread and some sliced beef. Then he left Lanny to eat it.

★   ★   ★

Hanna Blevins was later finishing her evening out than she had intended. She guessed that her brother Seth would soon be leaving to do his customary patrol of his domain, making sure that the drunks were not disorderly. That was why he usually ended up in a saloon. Hanna was not too happy walking alone through the street with so many rough miners in town, but she arrived back at the guest house safely enough, to find Seth just leaving.

'A fella come in, took that last bed,'

he told her. 'I fixed him up with some bread an' beef.'

She sighed. 'You should have given him something better than that.'

Seth departed, murmuring under his breath: 'Damn wimmin. A man can't do nothin' right!'

Hanna unpinned her hat, hung it up and went to the kitchen. Here she found everything as she had expected: bread and meat and butter left out, dirty knife on the table, the place in general disarray. Damn men, she thought, they can't do anything right.

She tidied up and then went to the dining room to make sure the new customer was satisfied. The two cribplayers had departed for their beds, and that just left the latecomer to chew on the rather stringy beef.

'Everything to your taste?' she enquired.

With his fingers, he picked a piece of meat from his tooth, then he turned. She felt dizzy with shock. She prided herself on never forgetting a face. And now, for a fleeting moment, she found herself looking into the dark eyes of a man she would always remember . . . the bank robber!

She turned immediately, went to Seth's gun rack in the kitchen and took down the only rifle in it — an old Remington slide-action model. Steeling herself, she rushed back to the dining room, pointing the heavy gun. Lanny was rising to his feet, wiping his lips.

'Put your hands up, mister,' she demanded, trying to make her voice firm.

He laughed. 'You wouldn't know how to pull the trigger, ol' woman!'

'My brother's the marshal,' she said. 'He'll lock you up.'

'He's gotta catch me first.' He had not raised his hands, nor did he appear to have any intention of doing so.

She tried to stem back her rising panic. For the first time in her life she wished that Seth was here. What could she do? She made up her mind. She would shoot this callous bandit, kill him if necessary. She pulled the trigger.

The rifle made a clicking sound.

He stepped forward, took hold of the barrel and wrenched the weapon from her grasp.

'You need to have ammunition in the gun, otherwise it ain't much good!' he said, then he lashed her across the face with the back of his hand, his chunky ring drawing blood. She was thrown backwards, knocking a chair aside as she collapsed. He looked at her, baring his teeth in a contemptuous smile. He debated whether he should kill her, but decided against it. To make sure she wouldn't trouble him further, he kicked his booted foot into her ribs.

He left the boarding house, stepping into the dark night, his mood foul. It was not safe to linger in Buffalo Springs any longer. He entered the next-door livery, relieved to find it still open. He led his gelded mustang from its stall and quickly saddled it, mounted and then rode out, leaving the open-mouthed hostler with his hand outstretched for the payment he would never get. Lanny figured he should have killed that old woman, but it was too late to go back now — and he had other urgent business requiring his attention.

It was a long ride to the homestead on Chippers Creek. He had covered a good stretch of the distance. But, urged by cruel spurring over rugged ground, and in darkness, Lanny's gelding was flagging. Suddenly its usual nimbleness failed it. Its left foreleg plunged through screening grass and found no purchase, causing it to lunge violently. Lanny was jerked from the saddle and hit the ground in an ungainly heap. Immediately, he scrambled up, cursing the animal as he glimpsed it hobbling off into the night. In anger, he drew his pistol and blazed a shot in its wake, missing by yards. He half started after it, but then realized the futility of such action. Although crippled, the gelding would easily outpace him. In the gloom he would never get anywhere near it.

In his fury he succumbed to a bout of

cursing, but after a while he cooled slightly. He would be obliged to proceed on foot, but he would help himself to a decent horse at the homestead. Meanwhile, his determination to avenge himself on his father and brother remained.

12

It was hours later and Hanna Blevins was hurting. Her ribs felt as though they were on fire and her face was painful. She wondered if she might die, but she dismissed the thought as anger surged through her. That terrible man had to be apprehended and punished at a rope's end. With a great effort, she forced herself to stand up. She tried to take a deep breath and groaned as agony shot through her chest. What a fool she had been not to check that the rifle had ammunition, but she had never previously handled firearms in her life. Where was Seth? She had to find him so he could give chase to that sonofabitch. She scolded herself for using such profane language, even in thought.

Clutching her ribs, she left the board-ing house, glancing furtively around to make sure her attacker was not lurking close by. Satisfied that he was gone, she walked totteringly along the darkened sidewalk. From the Lucky Ace, up the street, came the raucous sounds of voices and a squeeze-box. She shuddered. Normally she would not be seen dead in such a den of iniquity, but tonight she had to tell Seth what had happened. Soon she came to a spot where light spilled across the sidewalk from the saloon. A drunk, snoring loudly, was sprawled asleep by the doorway. She hesitated, then, picking up courage, she pushed her way through the batwings into the smoke-filled interior.

'Godstrewth,' a man cried out, 'it's Hanna Blevins!'

She was aware that all talking had died out. Even the squeeze-box had stopped. She was the focus of attention.

At last somebody said, 'Well, she sure looks like she's bin pulled through a thornbush backwards.'

She fought a bout of dizziness and her ribs were throbbing. She thought she might faint but she somehow remained upright.

One of the drinkers had put down his glass and was coming forward to offer her support, but she turned him back with a gesture of her hand. 'Where's my brother?' she managed to say. 'I've seen the fellow who robbed the bank. He attacked me. Seth must go after him.'

Her statement caused a burble of conversation, but it quieted when a squeaky voice sparked up and all eyes were drawn to a figure seated alone at a table — Kenny Tolly with a quarter-full glass of milk in front of him.

'The marshal ain't here, ma'am. He left me to keep order while he patrolled the back alleys.'

Hanna drew an exasperated hand across her brow. 'Then you'd better go and find him quick,' she said. 'Tell him I'll be waiting for him back home.'

'Yes, ma'am. Leave it to me.' Kenny Tolly stood up, finished his milk, walked to the door swinging his shoulders officiously and disappeared into the night.

The man who had recently offered Hanna support now stepped forward again and said, 'Ain't no time for a respectable lady to be out an' about. Let me escort you home, ma'am.'

She accepted his arm. She knew that the chances of catching the evil devil, yes, the sonofabitch, who had attacked her and was probably miles away by now, swallowed by the darkness, were nigh nonexistent.

★   ★   ★

Next morning, Brad and Mary-Ellen rose early, breakfasted, then, leaving baby Betsy in the capable care of Dan's wife Annie, they drove their buck-board wagon up to William Caulderfield's homestead. Pike's mare was quite at home between shafts. At the homestead, Brad dropped off his wife to attend to her daily chores, after which he headed for town, having been given a list of supplies needed by his father.

The church clock was striking ten as Brad pulled into Summerton. The place was smaller than Buffalo Springs but it served the local ranching communities well enough. Although past its glory days, it still retained a reasonable selection of amenities, including a good mercantile store. Brad hitched his wagon outside this, ensured the horse had easy access to the water trough, and went in, pulling out his shopping list.

He waited for a lady to finish her business, then staked his order.

'Ten pounds o' bacon an' ten pounds o' salt pork, five bags o' Arbuckle's, a dozen pounds o' flour, preferably without weevils, three dozen sticks o' Mexican vanilla, ten cans of evaporated milk, two sacks o' chilli beans, three jars o' plum jam, a dozen tins o' beans, four tins o' baccy, a half-dozen boxes of therapeutic papers, the sort without splinters, and that'll do.'

The shopkeeper had been listing the

items at speed. Now he put his pencil behind his ear and busied himself drawing together the supplies, much of which he packed in flour sacks.

Brad paid up and ferried his purchases on to the wagon, tying a tarpaulin over them for security. The sun had now turned into a fiery ball and he had worked up a considerable thirst, so he went across to the Fighting Rooster saloon and downed a couple of beers. The place was nigh deserted at this time of day apart from a thin, tired-looking woman in a torn dress, who reminded him of a chicken. She sidled up, offering her services and saying, 'A gal's got to make a livin',' but he shook his head.

Presently, he left the saloon and was crossing the street when he encountered, walking the opposite way, a dumpy little man wearing spectacles and dressed like a fancy gunslinger. He had a badge pinned to his vest, and was striding along swinging his shoulders, looking as if he owned the town. Shock took Brad's breath away as he realized this man was a deputy from Buffalo Springs. To his utter relief, Kenny Tolly, who was in Summerton to visit an ailing aunt, stepped straight past him, not sparing a sideways glance, as short-sighted as ever.

But the little fella's presence reminded Brad that he was not safe anywhere and he determined to be more careful in future.

* * *

Like a lobo drifting in from the wild, Lanny had reached the Caulderfield smallholding about the time Brad was halfway to Summerton. He was weary from his long walk, but the excitement pulsing through his veins overrode it, and his pace quickened as he passed the corral and the half-completed barn. He approached the house. Climbing on to the veranda, he noticed that the main door was open. As his eyes adjusted to the shadowy interior, he grunted with satisfaction.

The old man was sitting at the table, reading a newspaper, unaware he had a visitor. Lanny decided to play him along for a while.

'Hi, Pa,' he said.

His father looked up, starting with surprise. He rose to his feet, his chair pushed back.

'My God. Lanny!' he cried hoarsely.

'Ain't you glad to see your long-lost son?' Lanny said in a tone as soft as silk. 'I said I'd come back, didn't I? I've come back to say I'm sorry for the trouble we had.'

From the kitchen came the rattle of pans and Lanny guessed Mary-Ellen was there, unaware that he'd come home.

William Caulderfield had long imagined he would shoot his younger son if he showed up, but he had been caught by surprise, and now here was Lanny revealing contriteness that he had never displayed before.

'Lanny, you've put that Lilith in the

family way, and Mulvaney's so mad he's goin' to kick us out of this homestead. That's unless you come back an' face up to your sins.'

'Why, Pa, I'll sure do that. I'll marry the gal. That should calm Mulvaney down.'

'You'd really do that?'

'God's truth,' Lanny said with apparent sincerity. He looked around. 'Where's Brad?'

'In town gettin' supplies.'

Lanny frowned and said, 'I was hopin' he'd be here.'

At that moment Mary-Ellen, still unaware of the visitor, came into the room carrying a jug of coffee. At the sight of Lanny, she blanched and nearly dropped the jug.

'Oh Lord,' she gasped. 'I never thought you'd come back.'

'Well, now I'm here, ain't you gonna offer me a cup o' coffee?'

His father hesitated. All his desire to kill Lanny had gone. He could hardly believe the change in his repenting son.

Surely, his prayers had been answered. Maybe there was good in the boy after all. And maybe Mulvaney would withdraw his threat.

'Sit down, Lanny,' he said.

Mary-Ellen placed the jug on the table and produced three cups. They were rattling because her hands were trembling. Lanny's dark eyes still scared her.

They all sat at the table and she poured the coffee. Lanny laughed at her unsteadiness. 'No need to worry, Mary-Ellen. I've come back to put everythin' right. Ain't no cause to worry.'

She did not believe him.

'Where've you bin, Lanny, all this time?' William Caulderfield asked.

Lanny sipped his coffee, wishing it was whiskey. 'Oh, earnin' myself a few dollars.'

His father had placed his days-old newspaper, the Summerton Tribune, in front of him. Lanny noticed that the main headline reported the bank raid in

Buffalo Springs. He pointed to it.

Quite softly he said, 'I did that!'

Both his father and Mary-Ellen gasped with astonishment.

'You what?'

Larry laughed at their shocked faces. 'I did that job,' he said. 'An' I'm right proud of it.'

After a moment of stunned silence, Mary-Ellen accused him. 'So you killed that bank man?'

'He was makin' a nuisance of himself,' Lanny said. 'An' I robbed a stage as well!'

Both his father and sister-in-law were dumbfounded with horror.

Lanny's eyes met Mary-Ellen's defiantly. His tongue flicked out, reptile like, and wetted his now unsmiling lips. Increased fear gripped Mary-Ellen's heart like a cold hand. *He means to kill us*, an inner voice warned her.

Lanny knew that the game he had been playing was over. He was tired of it anyway. His attention returned to his father and he was suddenly shouting.

'The truth is, Pa, I've always hated you. An' now it's pay-back time!'

His face had become a twisted mask of malevolence.

William Caulderfield's hopes had plummeted. He should have guessed it would be like this. His gaze swung to his rifle, which was leaning against the wall, well beyond his reach. In a hopeless voice, he said, 'Your ma and me always loved you, showed you every kindness despite your bad ways, but you've turned out a wicked killer! Now you say you've always hated me. What're you gonna do about it?'

'This!' Lanny shouted. He snatched his gun from its holster, aimed point blank at his father's head and pressed the trigger. The blast thundered through the room, entwining with the shrillness of Mary-Ellen's scream. William Caulderfield was thrown back from his chair, his brains slapping the wall before he hit the floor. He lay unmoving.

Mary-Ellen screamed again, terror in

her eyes. She ran to the body, knelt down and gazed at the bloody mess that had once been the head of someone she loved. She howled with anguish.

Lanny laughed again. 'At least the ol' man won't have to worry 'bout eviction now.'

'You bastard!' she spat at him. 'You'll kill me now, eh?'

'Not yet, my prissy little madam,' he said. 'I got somethin' better in store for you. But first there's work to do. Go get the kerosene. Two cans.'

'Get it yourself!' She swallowed hard, the acridity of gunsmoke stinging her throat.

'You know, Mary-Ellen,' he said, 'I like a woman with spirit, an' you look damn pretty when you're angry.' He glanced around. 'Mebbe I can find a drop o' whiskey in the cupboard. Don't worry 'bout fetchin' the kerosene. Never let it be said that Lanny imposes on a lady. I'll get it. I guess the stuff's in the kitchen, just like it always was.'

'What're you gonna do?' she cried out.

'Make sure this place burns real good. Give my ol' man a grand send-off.'

13

Three hours later Brad smelt smoke in the air. He urged the mare into a faster pace and the springs of the wagon creaked as they bounced over the rough trail. Within a few minutes he saw dark smoke staining the sky above where the smallholding lay. He groaned, his heart heavy with dread. He wondered if Mulvaney had run out of patience and had tried to drive the Caulderfields from his land.

Evidence of tragedy was clear long before he drew up some distance back from the smouldering ruin of the homestead. The heat coming from it scorched him as he approached on foot, drawing his bandanna over his face. He saw the blackened corpse, a crumpled heap close to what was left of the veranda steps — and recognition dawned on him. It was Dan Carter, the

Negro who had served them so faithfully for many years.

Now new fear gripped him. Where were Mary-Ellen and his father? Had they died in the blaze?

Even as he watched, the timbers of the roof crashed inward, creating an angry crackle of sparks.

He turned, hoping and praying that Mary-Ellen was safe in their own cabin five miles along the creek.

He drove the mare with reckless speed. It seemed an age before he reached his home, but everything about the place seemed quiet as he fell from the wagon and rushed inside. On entering the living room, the first sight that greeted him was that of Dan's wife, Annie Carter, emerging from the bedroom cradling baby Betsy in her arms.

'Is Mary-Ellen here!' he cried.

Her troubled eyes gave him all the answer necessary. 'No, Mr Brad.'

He said, 'Oh, God!' and turned away as tears blurred his vision.

After a moment he swung back and half sobbed, 'Did you know Pa's homestead has been burned?'

She shook her head, horror building in her face.

'Nobody could've survived in that inferno,' he said. And now he knew he must give her the terrible news of Dan's death.

Choking back his own grief, he told her as gently as he could. She passed him the baby to hold, then she wept. Her tears came in great sobs that racked her body. Cradling the baby on his left arm, he hugged on to her plump shoulders with his right and they shared their grief. It occurred to him that Danny had not died because of the fire. His body was lying outside the house. Brad's anger against Mulvaney grew. 'He'll pay for what he's done,' he swore to himself.

As soon as was fitting Brad unloaded his supplies, left Annie and Betsy and drove back to the gutted homestead. Smoke still hung heavily in the air, but the extreme heat had diminished and he was able to reach Dan Carter. The Negro was sprawled on his back, already attracting flies, and Brad straight away saw the cause of his death: a bullet between the eyes.

Gingerly, he went forward, stepping among the charred and smouldering timber, the remnants of furnishings and the scattered possessions that had made up the home. He found the blackened remains of another human body — nothing more than a scorched skeleton — but instinct told him that this was his father and renewed fury surged through him.

He carried out a desperate search until it was dark, singeing his clothing and boots, burning his hands, not caring for his own safety. Presently, he gathered up Dan's body, and then the pitiful remains of his father, and laid them in the wagon. At least he would ensure they had a burial.

As he returned to his own cabin, hope warmed him. He felt certain that

Mary-Ellen's body had not been amid the devastation that had once been the homestead. But where was she?

That night he dug graves for his father and Dan on a grassy knoll overlooking his cabin. He buried them wrapped in blankets while Annie held a lantern and wept. They spoke a few words from the Bible and spent a time in remembrance. He knew it was not safe for him to venture into town and arrange a church burial. Perhaps when things were sorted out he would do it. Presently they went to their beds.

But sleep was out of the question. His mind wrestled with the awful, senseless events that had taken place. He saw his father's face, gaunt and worried about a future that would never be. He saw Mary-Ellen's sweet smile and prayed that she was somewhere safe and that she would come back to him.

Before he left, he set free the chickens and pigs. They would have to find their own food for the time being.

Next morning he rose before dawn. He hadn't the stomach for breakfast but drank a cup of strong coffee. He was tremulous with fury. If anybody knew where his wife was, it would be those who had fired the homestead. He strapped on his gun. Somebody must pay for the crime.

He saddled the mare and rode out for the Mulvaney ranch.

★　★　★

As Lanny had bundled Mary-Ellen out of the burning house, Dan Carter, having seen Lanny arrive and sensing trouble, had eventually come up from the cornfield in which he'd been working. Without warning, Lanny had gunned him down.

Lanny took two animals from the smallholding's corral, and saddled them. He told Mary-Ellen that if she attempted to run away, he would catch her and slash the tendons of her heels so that she could no longer walk, let alone run. She noticed that he had a knife sheathed on his belt.

As the cabin roared with fire behind them, scarlet and amber flames leaping skywards, she had thought of her father-in-law, who had always been kind to her, and now his body was being consumed by a furnace. And poor Danny Carter, when coming to help, he had been rewarded with death. She shuddered. She felt sure that she, too, would die soon.

Lanny had forced her to mount. It took three attempts because her legs were trembling so much. Then he had taken some rawhide string, which he had found in the barn, and lashed her feet tightly to the stirrups. Her horse was snubbed to his by a short rope. She gazed into the distance, hoping that Brad might appear to rescue her, but he did not. When they set off, Lanny didn't look back or speak.

They had ridden for what seemed an eternity, though she had no accurate way of telling the time, apart from the fact that it grew dark. Several times they stopped at streams to let the animals drink, but Lanny did not untie her so that she might refresh herself. He had found a bottle of whiskey at the homestead, and every few minutes he took a drag on it, eventually tossing the bottle away when he'd drained the last drop.

Her legs felt weak and numb. She closed her eyes and tried to sleep, but the fear in her was too acute, causing her head to throb. And all the while she was haunted by the nightmare she'd experienced.

Eventually they entered rocky terrain and crossed several dry gulches. Everywhere was given a ghostly sheen by the moon and stars. When Lanny dismounted he turned to her and she saw his teeth glint in a wolfish grin.

'We've arrived,' he said. 'My hideout. We won't be disturbed here.'

He had brought her to this, his secret place. He was certain about one thing: after he had finished with her, she would not leave here alive!

He was annoyed that Brad hadn't been at the homestead, hadn't suffered a fate he deserved. But he would get at his brother in a way even more punishing than a quick death — by the despoiling of his prissy wife. And he would make certain that Brad knew about it before he killed him.

Mary-Ellen noticed that they had entered a narrow canyon. He dismounted, came to her, took the knife from the sheath at his belt, and cut the strings that fastened her feet to the stirrups. He sheathed the knife and then tugged at her leg, pulling her from the horse's back, half-catching her as she fell. He roughly lowered her to the ground, then dragged her to her feet. He pushed her up some steps, on to a flat area.

'You ain't gonna run away, my darlin'',' he whispered to her, and she knew he was right, for her legs were utterly numb. 'Right now,' he added, 'I need a drink.'

He left her and entered his bush shelter. After a moment a lantern flared. She heard a bottle being uncorked followed by the gulping sound of his swallow. He was still holding the bottle when he returned. He loomed over her and she smelt the whiskey on his breath. She trembled and he laughed mockingly.

'No need to be scared, darlin',' he said. 'We're gonna have fun, for sure.' He took a long swig from his bottle. 'Get up,' he ordered.

She attempted to rise, but fell back. The numbness in her legs was wearing off and was replaced with pain. He growled impatiently, leaned forward, hooked his free hand under her armpit and dragged her up. He pulled her into the shelter, and in the dim light of the lantern, she saw a pallet. The smell of kerosene and whiskey filled her nostrils. He forced her down on the pallet. 'Now, darlin', you'll enjoy this. I'll be better than Brad, you'll see.'

He took off his belt and laid it to one

side. He removed his boots and socks, then he unbuttoned his pants and pulled them down. She screamed as he threw himself on top of her, crushing her. He clamped his hand across her mouth. 'I want you lively,' he stated, his voice slurred.

She wasn't lively. She closed her mind to him. He was like a wild animal and she hadn't the strength to resist him. His breathing was raucous. He hurt her with his roughness, but she clenched her eyes shut and didn't cry out again. She prayed over and over that she would survive.

After what seemed an age he was satiated and he rolled from her.

She felt ruined and soiled. He reached for the whiskey and gulped it down, long and hard. Sweat glistened on his brow.

She opened her eyes, for a moment focusing on the kerosene lamp that glowed from above. Then her gaze swung to him. He was seated, his legs spread before him, the bottle in his hand. He was still breathing heavily.

'That'll teach Brad a lesson,' he panted, taking another swig. 'His prim little woman ain't so prim now. He never treated me right, you know. Never talked to me, just looked down his nose at me and cosied up to Pa. Well, Pa has paid for favourin' him.'

Anger lifted her from her torpor. Her voice came husky and raw. 'He never favoured Brad. He gave you every chance, but you were too blind to see it.'

He laughed. He was maudlin and drunk. 'Weren't blind,' he mumbled. 'Just . . . didn't want to be bossed by Pa. As for Brad . . . he'll pay too, when I catch up with him. An' as for you . . . don't try to run away . . . Remember if you try . . . I'll slash your . . . pretty little ankles.' His final words came in a whisper. He closed his eyes. He lay back, rolled on to his side. After a moment he began to snore.

She felt she was being suffocated by the stench of whiskey and kerosene. A desperation came upon her. She sat up, wincing with the pain. Even had she wanted to run, she doubted she would have had the strength to do it. Perhaps there were other ways to escape him. She glanced around and saw the gunbelt lying on the ground where he'd discarded it. She was concerned about his heavy snoring. *Please God,* she thought, *don't let him wake himself up.*

She crawled to the gunbelt.

14

The mare was well lathered as Brad rode into the Bar B ranch-yard. He slid from the saddle, at the same time noticing that the door to the house was opening. Consuelo Mulvaney moved out on to the porch.

'Is my wife here?' Brad called.

'Your wife?' Consuelo responded as he ran towards her. 'No, *señor*. She ees not here. Why should she be?'

He stood at the base of the veranda steps, looking up at her, despair striking him like ice.

His voice came accusingly. 'Your husband set fire to my father's house, killed him an' our Negro servant!'

Her hand fluttered to her mouth with shock. 'No, *señor*, never. He would never do that. He swore he would evict you Caulderfields if Lanny didn't face justice, but not yet. Sam would not have killed your father, nor anybody else, except maybe Lanny.'

Brad groaned with frustration, feeling utterly defeated. Suddenly Lanny's words probed into his mind: *One day soon I'll come back an' I'll kill you both!*

And now a new terror hit him. Lanny must have taken Mary-Ellen!

'Sam's gone searching for Lanny,' Consuelo said. 'You see, Lilith told us that once Lanny took her to a secret place in the Cougat Hills, a canyon. She thinks that ees where he'll be hiding.'

'Why didn't she say so before?' Brad cried.

'Because she did not want to betray Lanny. He had promised that one day he would come for her, marry her and take her away.'

'Marry her!' Brad exclaimed.

'Yes . . . she still thought she loved him.'

'But he raped her.'

'No he did not,' Consuelo said. 'She only said that because she was afraid of her father. Afraid of what he might do if she told him her true feelings. This morning Sam was so angry with her. He threatened to whip her. She feared for herself and the baby inside her. She broke down, told heem everything. Now she has gone with heem to find Lanny. They left about an hour ago. I don't know what will happen.' Then she added, 'Señor Caulderfield, I am sorry about your father.'

He nodded and climbed back into his saddle. The Cougat Hills were ten miles north of Summerton. If Lanny had gone there, he must have taken Mary-Ellen with him — unless, God forbid, he'd killed her.

The mare had been sucking up water from the trough. She was already weary but he had to conserve what stamina she had left for the hard ride ahead. He waved his thanks to the Mexican woman and left the ranch.

He would try to catch Mulvaney up. Maybe they might not be travelling too fast as the girl was heavily pregnant. On the other hand, her father, being the merciless bully that he was, might not pander to her condition. Even making her ride was cruel.

As he travelled, Brad tried to make sense of what Consuelo had told him. Of course Lanny might not have gone to his hideout, might have lingered near the homestead in the hope of fulfilling his pledge to kill Brad. But he tried to push that possibility from his mind.

Lilith could have saved lives if she had revealed all she knew when her father had first discovered her outrageous behaviour. It was difficult to understand the girl's love for Lanny. He must have shown her a side of his character that he'd never displayed to his family. Or maybe he was a good actor. That day when she and her father had come to the homestead, fear of her father's reaction had prevented Lilith from admitting that she had welcomed Lanny's advances, in fact that she had enjoyed his passion. Instead, she had claimed that he had raped her. Ever since, she must have cherished her misguided adoration for Lanny, believing his promise that one day he would return, be a father to her child and spirit them away to a new life.

But now Mulvaney had extracted a confession from his daughter, had browbeaten her in to agreeing to betray Lanny.

* * *

Seth Blevins and Walking Hawk, only slightly inebriated, were on their way to the Caulderfield homestead in the hope of catching Brad or perhaps finding some clue as to his whereabouts by questioning the father. They had obtained special permission from the marshal in Summerton to carry out their investigations in his district.

They saw buzzards circling in the sky off to the west and decided to take a look. Fifteen minutes later they discovered what had attracted the birds — a half open grave. As they approached three coyotes took fright, ran off a short distance and sat watching.

'Coyotes must've been diggin',' Blevins opined.

They dismounted and looked down through a cloud of flies into the hole. The marshal grunted with distaste at the sight of a half-excavated, decomposing corpse. The foul stench of it hit them and they hoisted their bandannas over their noses.

'Him mighty big man,' Walking Hawk remarked.

Blevins eyed the gaping wound in the man's guts. It was seething with maggots. 'Been shot,' he said. 'Looks like another victim of Caulderfield. Somethin' else for him to account for when we catch him.' He fanned away the flies that had taken a liking to his sweating face.

'Him mighty big man,' Walking Hawk repeated.

Blevins ignored his revulsion and took a closer look at the corpse. When he straightened up, he said, 'That's

Algernon Pike. I'm certain of it.'

Walking Hawk nodded.

'It's pointless coverin' the body again,' Blevins commented. 'The coyotes'll only dig it up. Let's ride for the homestead. Mebbe we'll find a few answers.'

As they left the grave, the coyotes slunk back.

When the two riders reached the homestead, they were shocked to find a burned-out ruin.

★　★　★

The tiny settlement of Silverwood straddled the trail that ran from east to west. It boasted five buildings: a blacksmith's forge, three shacks and a store which doubled up as a saloon, the pride of which was a fine brass spittoon. The settlement supported the occasional traveller passing through, and the few local farmers and cowboys who came for supplies and to quench their thirst.

When Brad rode in the mare was flagging. He left her at the water trough outside the store and entered the place. A rotund man with huge sideburns greeted him from behind the counter and supplied him with a lukewarm beer drawn from a keg.

'Have any folks passed through?' Brad enquired. 'A gal was with 'em.'

The storekeeper nodded. 'About an hour ago. That gal looked as if she was about to drop a young 'un. I guess the ridin' shook her up. Ain't right for a gal in her condition to be astride a hoss.'

Brad took a quick sip of his beer.

'It's been the busiest day we've had in years,' the storekeeper went on. 'Earlier, we had another woman ride in. She looked right poorly an' she had blood on her hands.'

'Where is she now?' Brad gasped.

'Ol' Widow Harrowsmith is lookin' after her. Second house down on the left.'

Brad uttered his thanks as sudden hope surged through him. He rushed from the store to the shack indicated.

The door stood open and he rapped

on it with his knuckles. A plumpish, grey-haired woman answered. 'Yes?'

'I'm lookin' for my wife,' Brad got out.

At that moment a cry sounded and Mary-Ellen appeared from inside the shack. She threw herself into Brad's arms.

'Well, I guess you found her!' Mrs Harrowsmith exclaimed.

'Thank God you're here,' Mary-Ellen gasped.

For a while Brad held her, feeling sobs course through her body.

'You're safe now, my love,' he soothed her, but her weeping continued.

'Is Betsy all right?' she asked anxiously.

'She's fine. Poor Annie's takin' good care of her. She's grievin' hard for Dan. She said it was good to have the baby to take her mind off things.'

After a moment she said, 'Lanny kidnapped me. He . . . he murdered your pa and Dan Carter and set fire to the homestead. He took me to his hideout and then he . . . he . . . '

168

'Don't torture yourself,' he whispered, smoothing her hair. 'Sit down, honey.' He led her to a chair.

'He was so drunk,' she went on, 'but I got away from him and found his horse. I rode until I came to the trail that led here. Mrs Harrowsmith has been real kind to me.'

'Mrs Harrowsmith,' Brad said, 'we're mighty grateful to you.'

'It was my pleasure, dear,' came the response. 'She was so distressed, and she kept saying she wanted a doctor. Not for herself, mind you. For somebody else. We don't have no doctor here. The nearest thing is the blacksmith, Henry Judson. He claims he delivered a baby once.'

'Who did you want a doctor for?' Brad asked.

'For Lanny,' she replied. 'He might be bad hurt.'

'He deserves to be,' he said. 'I guess I owe him a thing or two.'

'Well, I reckon the best we can offer is Henry,' Mrs Harrowsmith said. 'I'm sure he'll be glad enough to come out.'

Mary-Ellen looked full of gloom. 'Brad,' she said. 'I've done something terrible.'

'Mebbe the lady could rest here,' Mrs Harrowsmith said, turning to Brad. 'You best come with me and explain the situation to Henry.'

'Yup, I'll do that. I'd like a fresh hoss. Mine's tuckered out.'

Within fifteen minutes Brad had exchanged the mare for a sprightly young chestnut and swapped over his saddle on to it. He told himself he would come back for the mare after she'd had a good breather and a sackful of oats.

Just then Mary-Ellen came into the blacksmith's forge. 'I couldn't rest,' she said. 'I don't want to let you out of my sight, ever again.'

'Honey, I'm going after Lanny.'

She sighed. 'He'll be dangerous.'

'I'll take care.'

'Then I'm going with you, Brad. I've got a fair idea where the hideout is.'

'But you ain't fit enough, honey.'

'Try me!' There was a defiant expression on her face.

He could see she was not going to back down. Furthermore, if she could lead him to the hideout, it would be useful. Of course it was far from certain that Lanny would still be there, but it was a chance he had to take. Anyway, Mulvaney was somewhere ahead of him, and Brad felt a desperate urge to reach Lanny before he did.

Henry Judson, a brawny, hairy-armed man, pointed out the horse that Mary-Ellen had been riding when she arrived at the settlement. Brad recognized the animal. It had belonged to his father. Lanny must have taken it. Brad soon had it saddled.

Despite what she said, his wife was still weak, but he helped her up on to the horse. Meanwhile, Henry Judson had agreed to accompany them, and, having bidden farewell to Mrs Harrowsmith, the three of them headed out of Silverwood.

15

For fifteen minutes they followed back along the route which Mary-Ellen had taken, passing through forest, until they reached a point when she said they should leave the trail. They now hit open ground which undulated in dips and swells and led up to a line of rocks and foothills beyond. These were the Cougat Hills. Brad's heart quickened as he realized that Lanny might be hidden somewhere up there.

But suddenly they heard the burble of voices. Topping a swell in the ground, they reined in and gazed down into a dip to see a group of people: Sam Mulvaney, three of his ranch hands, and young Lilith. They had all dismounted, the horses standing near by. The girl was lying on a blanket and her groans carried clearly.

'Glory be!' Mary-Ellen exclaimed.

'She must be having her baby.'

They urged their horses down into the dip, and Mulvaney's distraught face turned towards them. Lilith's cries were growing desperate.

'What a damn time to decide to give birth,' Mulvaney grunted.

'I don't reckon she had any choice,' Brad said. 'You forced her to come.'

Mulvaney scowled but said nothing. Brad and Henry Judson dismounted, and Brad helped Mary-Ellen from her saddle.

'One thing's for sure,' Mary-Ellen said. 'She don't want a load of menfolk standing round gawping. Get a fire lighted, boil some water, and let Lilith have a little privacy.'

All the males present mumbled but shuffled off out of the hollow, except for the blacksmith, who claimed he had experience in childbirth. He drew together some brush and started a fire. He then emptied several canteens into a skillet and set it to boil.

Lilith had obviously gone into labour,

but no baby had been born yet or appeared to be imminent and she was no longer groaning.

Brad thanked God that he had Mary-Ellen along, and even Henry Judson might prove helpful.

He took his sougan and blanket from the back of his horse and carried them down to where his wife was comforting the girl. Mary-Ellen thanked him and spread them over Lilith. They smelt downright horsey but it was the best they had.

'This might take hours,' Mary-Ellen said, rubbing the back of her hand across her brow. He nodded and returned to his place beyond the hollow.

Hours, he thought. Lanny could be miles away before they found his hideout. Yet, clearly, Mary-Ellen could not leave Lilith in her present state. He gazed at the close-by hills. Without either of the women they would never trace the hideout.

Mulvaney came to where Brad was

hunkered down. He was champing at the bit. 'It's as if that sonofabitch is playin' a game with us. Putting Lilith in the family way to slow us up, so he can get away. I'll go and speak to your wife, see if she'll leave her and let Nature take its course.'

'You'll do no such thing,' Brad retorted. 'Lilith's life and the baby's are more important than catching my brother. I know what your daughter did was bad, but she's still your flesh and blood and you've got to show her consideration.'

Mulvaney cursed, but Brad's words struck a cord. He slumped to the ground, muttering, and sat with his head in his hands. Brad was equally frustrated. He wanted to bring Lanny to justice as much as Mulvaney did, but they were hogtied and all they could do was wait.

The heat had gone out of the day; the sky settled into a low grey ceiling of cloud and it began to rain, a depressing drizzle. The ranch hands sat around smoking, playing cards and looking miserable. Soon, they wrapped themselves in their sougans.

An hour passed, then they all heard Lilith scream three times. They waited with bated breath for further sound. It seemed that silence prevailed for an eternity. Suddenly they all heard the unmistakable sound of a baby crying. They came to their feet, exhaling with relief.

Brad said, 'I'll take a look.' He ran to the edge of the wallow and stared down. He saw Mary-Ellen wrapping a baby in a blanket. It reminded him of the joyous moment when he had first held Betsy. He rushed down, and the others followed him. Mary-Ellen was smiling. 'The babe's come early,' she said. 'It's a little gal, and Lilith is all right, thank God.'

'Let me see,' Mulvaney said, and Mary-Ellen handed him the child.

He held her awkwardly, and for a moment the suggestion of a smile flitted across his face. 'The image of her ma,' he said. He handed the bundle back to Mary-Ellen who rested her against her mother's breast. Lilith looked pale and washed out, but she took the baby and hugged on to her as if she never intended to leave go.

'She must rest now,' Mary-Ellen said. 'She's certainly not fit enough to travel.' She rearranged the sougan which protected the girl from the rain. Meanwhile Henry Judson had buried the afterbirth.

'We gotta push on,' Mulvaney stated, his fleeting tenderness gone. He turned to Mary-Ellen. 'Mrs Caulderfield, I'll be obliged if you'll accompany us and show us how to get to the hideout.'

'D'you think you can find it?' Brad asked his weary wife. She nodded and said that Lilith, during her more relaxed moments, had tried to explain the way. The girl was still terrified of her father and what he might do to her if she failed to cooperate.

Mulvaney detailed a man to stay with his daughter and look after her until she was strong enough to get to Silverwood where she and the baby could rest.

Brad, Mary-Ellen, Henry Judson, Mulvaney and two of his men, Windy Turnpike and Bos Oliver, went to their horses, got mounted up and shortly they were crossing the prairie towards the Cougat Hills.

Twenty minutes later found them threading their way through deep, shadowy canyons and dry gulches. Ground squirrels scattered before them. The clip-clop of hoofs echoed alarmingly. The light was fading fast and the drizzle persisted, dampening their spirits. As they rode, Brad scanned the high rims that surrounded them. He wondered if Lanny might be up there somewhere, watching them with his gun ready. On the other hand, with Mary-Ellen having escaped him, he was more likely to have put as much distance as he could between this place and some safe haven.

Mulvaney pressed them for greater haste, as if every passing second lessened his chances of satisfying the lust for revenge that burned through his soul.

Mary-Ellen had kept going despite her exhaustion, but Brad was concerned for her as she strove to guide them through the canyons. She'd been through a terrible ordeal and he swore to himself that he must never let it happen again.

Before long, she pulled in beside him and murmured, 'I guess we're here.'

They all drew rein and gazed at the surrounding terrain. Everything was silent, apart from the eerie squawks of ravens on the rock faces high above them. They were in a canyon with steep sides, and on the left there was a natural path that led into a dark recess.

'This is the ideal place for a damn trap,' Mulvaney commented in a hushed voice. Brad agreed.

As if in confirmation of their opinion, a heavy calibre shot boomed out. It set up an echo in the canyon like a dam bursting, and aroused renewed screeching from the birds. With a desperate cry, Brad urged Mary-Ellen to ride on. Turning, he saw that Mulvaney had been thrown from his horse and was sprawled on his back, his animal taking flight. The two ranch hands had also moved further into the canyon, unaware that their boss had been hit. Henry Judson turned back to help Brad, but Brad waved him away, gesturing for him to take cover with the others and he complied. They found refuge behind some clumps of mesquite close up against the rock wall.

Brad wheeled his chestnut and galloped back to Mulvaney. He dismounted, struggling to maintain a grip on the reins of his agitated mount. The rancher was groaning and clutching his left shoulder, a crimson stain showing through his fingers. The fall, too, had clearly shaken him up, but now his eyes were full of alarm as he realized he was an easy target for a second shot.

He pushed himself into a sitting

position and Brad gripped him under the armpit of his good shoulder. He was wincing with pain as Brad hauled him to his feet. At that moment another shot boomed out. This time the bullet struck head-high and close in to the left, sending splinters of rock through the air.

Heads down, the two men moved forward, the horse proving an unintended shield. As they joined the others in the mesquite cover, three more shots came, but were well wide of the mark.

Unbidden, Mary-Ellen had ripped off part of her skirt. Brad helped Mulvaney struggle out of his shirt, and they got the bandage around the wound, and bound it tightly, hoping that the bleeding would be stemmed. There was no way of telling if the bullet had lodged inside, but the rancher was fit enough to curse vociferously.

Not once during the barrage of shots had they been able to determine where their assailant was hidden. Brad knew that the screen of mesquite would provide little protection from further bullets, but at least it concealed them. He was worried about the horses. They stood behind them, clearly in view as future targets.

The two ranch hands, Windy Turnpike and Bos Oliver, together with Henry Judson, had gathered together some small rocks, heaping them to form a slight barricade, and Mary-Ellen had joined them behind this.

Mulvaney sat beside Brad, breathing heavily. 'What're we gonna do?' he said. 'Mebbe Lanny has pulled out. Things've gone quiet.'

Brad nodded. He studied the rock face on the other side of the canyon, but it revealed nothing. 'When it's dark,' he said, 'I'll go over and take a look.'

'I guess I should come with you.'

'You can't,' Brad said. 'Not wounded like you are.'

Mulvaney uttered a deep sigh. 'I feel so goddamn helpless,' he said.

They waited and the darkness seeped

into the canyon. The ravens had quieted, but coyotes sent their yip-yap cries into the night and the horses, still nervous, emitted occasional blowing sounds.

Brad crept back to where Mary-Ellen, Turnpike, Oliver and Judson sheltered and satisfied himself that they were reasonably safe, although they had exhausted their water supplies and they were all thirsty.

'I'm goin' across and see if I can find Lanny,' Brad said. 'He may have pulled out, in which case we could stay here for hours for nothin'.'

Mary-Ellen voiced alarm. 'He'll be waiting for you Brad. I'm sure of it. There's something I should tell you. Something I'm so ashamed of.'

'Tell me when I get back. Don't worry. You have nothin' to be ashamed of. I'll be careful, honey.' He leaned forward and gave her a kiss on the forehead. Her hand gripped his until he gently pulled away. Then he moved off.

He returned to where Mulvaney sat

and was about to leave the mesquite cover when the rancher reached out and touched his arm. 'I owe you a big thank you, Caulderfield,' he whispered. 'You saved my life.'

'I guess you'd have done the same for me,' Brad responded. He rose to his feet and was on his way.

The darkness was not as deep as he would have wished. He moved over the canyon floor at a brisk pace, careful to avoid the small rocks that were scattered about. For what seemed an age, he knew he was an easy target and he was tensed in expectation of the gun booming again, but it did not and he reached the mesquite-clogged far side. He crouched down and steadied his heaving breath.

He was at the point where the narrow opening split the cliff-face. He edged into it, drawing his gun. That was when he slipped on the wet shale and fell, causing a rattling of rocks. He cursed, knowing that all chance of surprise was lost. Maybe now, Mary-Ellen was right.

Lanny would be waiting for him. That was if he was near.

He went forward again, and that was when the smell of equine urine became evident. He found himself in a small enclosure of rock. It must have been used as a shelter for horses, although there was none here now.

Fumbling in the darkness, he came across some steps chipped out of the rock. He mounted them. He paused at the top — and gasped. He could just make out the brush shelter and knew that he had found Lanny's hideout. But where was Lanny?

Then he heard the slight clink of a bottle against the rock and realized that the air was tainted with the smell of whiskey.

He approached the brush shelter, peered inside but everything was in darkness. He felt sure, however, that nobody was in the shelter. He shuddered as he realized that this was where Lanny had brought Mary-Ellen, where he had violated her. His grip on his gun tightened as he moved around the shelter, went forward a few paces, and saw the ledge. Seated on the ledge, overlooking the canyon and behind a balustrade of rocks, was a shadowy figure. Instinct warned Brad that he had found Lanny.

16

He aimed his gun at Lanny, knowing that right now he could kill him. Despite his anger at what his brother had done to Mary-Ellen, he couldn't bring himself to pull the trigger. Instead, he called out: 'Lanny! It's me, Brad.'

He had expected his brother to twist around, gun first, and he would have shot him then. But Lanny stayed facing outward, his words coming in a slurred wheeze.

'I knew you'd come, Brad. I could've killed you before, but I'm out of shells. Now I guess I'm at your mercy.' He paused, talking was a struggle for him. When he'd recovered his breath he went on: 'I'd like it if we could kinda forgive each other for past wrongs. Let's let bygones be bygones.'

'I can never forgive you, Lanny, for

murderin' Pa, and for what you did to Mary-Ellen.'

'Well, I guess that your bitch of a wife got more than her own back on me.' His voice had dropped to a bitter whisper. 'She's left me in agony. It was as much as I could do to drag myself to this ledge. I'll never walk again, not properly. If it was daylight you'd see the blood on the rocks where I dragged myself along.'

'Why? What happened?' Brad didn't trust his brother one iota.

Lanny swallowed hard, then said, 'She cut the tendons on my heels. Then she walked out and left me, and there was nothin' I could do about it. The pain's awful. It's killin' me. If it hadn't been for the whiskey, I'd've gone crazy. Now it's all gone.'

Brad gasped with astonishment. He edged closer, keeping his Colt up. Lanny did not turn. He was sitting with his legs splayed before him, a rifle alongside. Brad glanced down at Lanny's feet, but they were completely in shadow. He picked up the rifle. True enough the magazine was empty. He cast the weapon aside.

'And there's somethin' else,' Lanny gasped. 'The other side o' the shelter there's a hole with a slab of rock over it. In the hole is a fortune in bank notes. Take it, Brad, all of it. All I ask in exchange is that you get me out of this mess. Help me, an' we'll go up north, leave all this behind us.'

Brad's response came in three hissed words: 'Go to hell!'

Taking a chance, he thrust his own gun into its holster, then he cupped his hands to his mouth and called to those on the other side of the canyon. He called that it was safe for them to leave their cover and join him in Lanny's hideout.

*　　*　　*

Mary-Ellen did not want to return to the hideout. It was a place of her worst nightmare, but Mulvaney and his man,

Bos Oliver, crossed over the canyon and climbed to where Brad and Lanny waited.

When Mulvaney saw Lanny he was unable to restrain his anger. He drew his gun, would have shot him, but Brad knocked the weapon aside before he could fire.

'A quick death's too good for him,' Brad said, 'after all the evil he's done. He must have a fair trial, remindin' him o' his terrible sins and knowin' that the hang-rope is waitin' for him.'

'I guess you're right,' Mulvaney grudgingly agreed.

At last Lanny turned his head, unaware of how close he had come to taking a bullet. His face was twisted with pain, and he was letting out a low, continuous groan.

'Mary-Ellen slashed the tendons of his heels,' Brad explained. 'Just like the Comanche used to do. He ain't goin' nowhere now, not on his own feet.'

'Mary-Ellen!' Mulvaney exclaimed. 'Slashed his damn heels? Well I'll be goddamned.' He spat to emphasize his contempt. 'No more than the sonofa-bitch deserved. I guess all the sufferin' he's havin' will do him good. He'll go to the gallows in a wheelchair, eh?'

The night dragged on. Lanny had lapsed into a restless sleep, unleashing shouts from time to time, no doubt tortured by some nightmare. Mulvaney retired to the bush shelter and lit a lamp.

Presently Brad left Oliver to watch over Lanny and crossed back across the canyon where he found a relieved Mary-Ellen and Windy Turnpike waiting.

He briefly told them what had happened.

When he finished, Mary-Ellen said, 'Brad, you know what I did now? You know I cut his heels. It was a terrible sin. I have asked God's forgiveness. That's why I wanted to get a doctor to him, to in some way redeem myself.'

Brad nodded. He couldn't quite understand her reasoning.

'You did what you had to,' he said.

'Nothin' to be ashamed of. Tell me, honey, how did you manage it?'

She seemed to choke back on her breathing, then her words came slowly. 'He got so drunk, he went to sleep. I got to his belt. His knife was in a sheath on it. I took it out. He was lying on his side, his back to me, his heels exposed. The knife was so sharp. It was easy to slice the tendons. He woke up, yelled out. He made a grab for me but I got away. He tried to chase me, but he screamed with pain and collapsed. Thank God he did. I found the horses, got mounted on one and set the other free. I rode like crazy and got to Silverwood.'

She was crying. She appeared drained by confessing what she considered to be a terrible sin, yet he would forever see it as justifiable retribution. He took her in his arms and did his best to soothe her. He knew what Lanny had done to her, and the knowledge turned to bitter anger.

When dawn showed its glimmer above the canyon rims, the rain ceased. Brad returned to the hideaway.

Windy Turnpike had found some supplies of pemmican and water in the brush shelter and they all allayed their immediate needs. Lanny was awake, moving only slightly to relieve himself. He maintained a morose silence, but his eyes, smouldering with resentment, followed Brad.

Mulvaney and Oliver searched up-canyon and recovered the horses, which had galloped off in panic. The rancher's wound had stopped bleeding, though the bandage was heavily stained, but it did not appear to be troubling him unduly. Meanwhile Brad and Windy Turnpike fashioned a primitive travois from mesquite branches. Lanny was carried down from the hideout in Henry Judson's great blacksmith's arms and secured to the travois. His feet hung loosely at a grotesque angle. By nine o'clock the little procession was ready to move out. With the exception of Lanny, they left the canyon with few regrets. Mary-Ellen kept well away from Lanny, not favouring him with a single glance.

The sun was hot when they reached Silverwood. There they found Lilith, the baby and their protecting ranch hand at Mrs Harrowsmith's. The widow had cared for them well. Lilith was much brighter and the baby was gurgling.

They all fed at Silverwood's store and Brad gratefully traded in his mount for Pike's mare, for which he had considerable affection.

The entire party left at noon, having had Mulvaney's wound bathed and rebandaged. Lanny pleaded for whiskey but it was denied him.

In the late afternoon they pulled into Summerton and lodged Lanny at the marshal's jail. Brad was anxious in case he was recognized, but nobody paid much attention to him. He left the explaining to Mulvaney and the marshal reacted efficiently, saying he would notify the authorities at Buffalo Springs of events.

Afterwards, Mulvaney went off to find the doctor and get his wounded shoulder attended to, and the others left for home.

Brad was uncertain about what the future held. Clearly, the prospect of eviction no longer applied. With Lanny under lock and key awaiting the justice he so richly deserved, and the main Caulderfield homestead a burned-out ruin, Mulvaney would be satisfied, but the fact remained that Brad was still a wanted man.

His worse fears were realized when they pulled in at their cabin. All was quiet at first, too quiet, and he sensed trouble in the air. Wearily, they dismounted, hoping to be greeted, at the door, by Annie Carter and baby Betsy — but they were met by a sinister wall of silence.

And then came the metallic slotting of steel on steel as cocking pieces were levered, and a good half-dozen deputies emerged from the trees, all aiming their rifles at Brad. Marshal Seth Blevins was foremost amongst them.

'Brad Caulderfield,' he cried out, 'you're under arrest. I'm chargin' you with the murder of my brother!'

17

The dates for the twin trials of Lanny
and Brad Caulderfield were set at one
month after their arrests, and were to
take place in the Buffalo Springs
courthouse. Lanny was held in the cells
beneath the courthouse where his heels
were bound up by the doctor, although
there was no prospect of him ever
walking again. However nobody was
very much concerned.

Brad was held in the cells at Marshal
Blevin's office with an extra guard
on duty. Every day, Mary-Ellen came to
visit him, bringing food and books
to read, but he could not put his mind
to them. Another visitor was Jock
Wilberforce who came from the law
office in Buffalo Springs. He was to be
the attorney for the defence. He was an
alert, smartly dressed young man, a
sandy-haired Scot, lean and muscular.

He asked Brad many questions and took copious notes. They went over the whole story from start to finish. He queried with Brad whether he wished to testify himself and Brad shook his head. Unless he was called, he would let his attorney do the talking.

Seth Blevins carried out his work in the office, supervising guard duties, but he never spoke to Brad nor paid him any attention apart from ensuring that he was securely locked up.

The days slipped by and excitement in the town grew at the prospect of the approaching trials. At last Wilberforce had accrued all the evidence he could and he ceased his visits to the jail and retired to his office to prepare his case. He learned that Lanny, in an effort to avoid the severest punishment, had revealed the hiding place of his loot, which had been recovered.

Brad also learned that he, himself, was to be charged with two murders — those of Frank Blevins and Algernon Pike.

He lapsed into a heavy depression which even defied Mary-Ellen's attempts to raise his spirits. He felt sure the odds were stacked against him. Seth Blevins would do his utmost to ensure that.

In the moments that he was alone, Brad went over in his mind the events that had led up to his killing of Frank Blevins.

Still searching for his brother, he had ridden in to Buffalo Springs. Having drawn a blank yet again, he entered the saloon, got involved in a game of poker. He had hit a very substantial winning streak, relieving two ranchers of large sums of money. Afterwards he quit the saloon, and rode out of Buffalo Springs. It was now late at night and quite dark. After a while, he heard the blowing of a horse from somewhere behind him and guessed he was being followed.

Fearing he was in danger of being robbed of his winnings, he lit a small fire and rigged up his saddle and blanket beside it to give the impression of a sleeping man. He hid in the nearby trees. Some time later a number of shots rang out, all being fired into the saddle and blanket. Clearly the intent was murder. Brad stepped from his cover with his own gun drawn. He hailed the intruder who made no acknowledgement but raised his gun and fired. The bullet missed Brad. Expecting another shot, Brad pressed his trigger, shooting the other man through the heart.

Next morning he brought the corpse into the Buffalo Springs mortuary. He would not have done so had he believed he was a murderer. After this he went to the marshal's office and reported the matter to Blevins. He and Brad then went to the mortuary and Blevins identified the deceased as his brother. Deputies Kenny Tolly and Tom Evans were present at this time.

Brad showed the marshal the bullet-holed blanket, regarding it as proof that he had acted in self-defence.

At this point, Marshal Blevins suggested that Brad should accompany him to his office to complete some paperwork, his office being down the street. Brad agreed and the two of them did as suggested. But once there, Blevins drew his gun and stated that he was arresting Brad on a charge of murder. He relieved him of his weapon and motioned him to the adjoining cell. As he was unlocking the cell, he foolishly turned his back and Brad struck him a hard blow across the side of the head. While Blevins reeled, Brad bundled him into the cell, locked the door and pocketed the key. He then quit the office, recovered his horse and left town.

Later, he realized a posse was on his trail. But when he was crossing Devil's Ford, he ran foul of the snakes.

★   ★   ★

At last the day for the trials to commence arrived. Lanny's trial took place first. He was pushed in to court in a wheelchair. Brad remained confined, lying on his cot, waiting out the long hours. Through the tiny window near the roof of his cell, he could see that many folks had come in to town for the proceedings and numerous wagons and horsemen moved up and down the street. They all arrived despite the fact that heavy rains had come and everything seemed grey and dismal. It was all good for local trade.

After three days, Lanny's trial was over and he was wheeled back to his cell. Deputy Tom Evans informed Brad that the jury had reached a unanimous verdict: guilty of murder and armed robbery. Judge Morgan had delayed announcing the sentence until after the second Caulderfield brother had been tried, but that didn't stop the gallows being erected at the top of Main Street by local builders — a hewn beam stretched across a grotesque scaffold fifteen feet high.

Seventy-two hours later, Brad was led over to the courthouse for his trial, handcuffed and under heavy escort. He exchanged a nod with a pale-faced Mary-Ellen who was sitting at the back of the courtroom, which was already packed except for the two rows roped off for the jury. Several newsmen were in attendance.

Brad took his place at the defence table alongside Jock Wilberforce, conscious of the stares he attracted. At the table opposite sat Edward Sparkman and his team of prosecutors. Sparkman was a rotund man of about fifty with a high forehead and bald pate.

Everybody stood up as Judge Morgan strode in. He mounted his platform, sat down behind his great desk, and declared that the court was now in session and all could be seated. Morgan was a surprisingly short man, grey haired, and he wore pince-nez. The jurors took their places in the roped-off area and were sworn in. They consisted of local ranchers, farmers, a blacksmith and two retail merchants. They were all strangers to Brad.

Sparkman stood up and announced,

'The case for the prosecution is ready, your Honour,' and Judge Morgan nodded. He then read out the charges that Brad Caulderfield had murdered Frank Blevins and Algernon Pike and asked for a plea of guilty or not guilty.

'Guilty of manslaughter,' Brad replied.

Judge Morgan leaned forward and said, 'The charge is murder. Please respond to the charge.'

Brad consulted with Wilberforce and then announced, 'Not guilty, your Honour.'

The judge now called upon the prosecution to present its case. Sparkman rose and took centre stage. His voice was firm and convincing, but he got pulled up after only a few words. 'We have before us today, the second of the notorious Caulderfield brothers . . . '

'Objection!' Wilberforce cried. 'The prosecution has no right to link the brothers together or to call them notorious.'

'Objection upheld,' Judge Morgan responded. But the words used by

Sparkman left Brad uneasy. *The notorious Caulderfield brothers.* The seed had been sewn.

Sparkman continued as though he had not been rebuffed. 'Brad Caulderfield has already admitted to killing both Frank Blevins and Algernon Pike, claiming self-defence. With no witnesses in either case, it's too easy to claim self defence. So is it all too easy to claim he was attacked by both men. Any of us would make the same claims if we were on trial for murder. He is also guilty of evading arrest. Why would he have done that if he knew he was innocent? It is clear he stole another man's woman. But the most damning evidence of all comes from his brother Lanny, sworn under oath, that Brad Caulderfield persuaded him to rob both bank and stagecoach and that he gave advice as to how to go about it.'

The final comment brought a surge of excited murmurs in the court and the judge hammered with his gavel to restore order.

'I appeal to the jury,' Sparkman said, 'to ignore the fabricated evidence that the defence will present and to find this man guilty on two counts of first-degree murder. Your consciences will give you no other choice.'

The judge turned his gaze on the defence table and said, 'You may now deliver your opening remarks, Mr Wilberforce.'

The young attorney rose. He spoke briefly, countering most of what Sparkman had stated and concluding with emphasis on the two killings being in self-defence.

When Wilberforce sat down, Brad sensed a surge of feeling in the courtroom, a feeling that the case was going in favour of the prosecution.

Throughout the afternoon, proceedings continued. Sparkman gave a detailed and strongly biased account of the killings. He paced the well of the court, furthering the case to a damning conclusion. He called as witnesses Deputies Tom Evans and Kenny Tolly, both of whom had been present at the morgue when Brad had brought the body in. The courtroom rocked with laughter when the bespectacled, fancy dressed Tolly revealed that his full names were Kenneth Abraham Hirham Ebenezar Cornelius Tolly. Sparkman also called Seth Blevins. All corroborated details of Brad's escape.

When the prosecution rested its case, Wilberforce rose to speak for the defence. He stood in the centre of the well, feet apart, hands clasped behind his back. His voice came in a forthright manner.

'The claim that Brad Caulderfield advised his brother regarding robbery of stagecoach and bank is strongly denied. I would next like to go into events which led up to the killing of Frank Blevins. Blevins was not a man of strong character, but was a gambler and drinker. He was present in the saloon at the same time that Brad Caulderfield hit a very substantial winning streak at the poker table.'

Wilberforce then related how Frank Blevins had been killed, and how events had unfolded with Seth Blevins being locked in his own cell.

Brad looked over his shoulder and saw the marshal sitting three rows behind him, a sullen expression on his face.

'Blevins eventually got himself released,' Wilberforce said, 'and he immediately set out with his posse in pursuit of Caulderfield, but was prevented from catching him by a plague of grasshoppers. Caulderfield may well consider that running off was wrong, but with an accusation of murder levelled against him it was a natural reaction. However Fate was conspiring against him because he was bitten by a snake.'

Wilberforce next turned to the killing of Algernon Pike. He detailed the facts that Brad had given to him; Stella Goodnight had run away with him of her own free will. He had killed Pike in self-defence.

Finally Wilberforce called Seth Blevins

as witness. He asked him if Caulderfield had shown him the bullet-holed blanket. The marshal tried to prevaricate but Wilberforce nailed him into an admission that he had seen the blanket.

The young attorney stated that he had no further witnesses to call. However he added that in his opinion Blevins had been highly chagrined at having been locked in his own cell, so chagrined in fact that he had sworn to have Caulderfield indicted for murder.

'Your Honour,' Wilberforce concluded, 'I move for the dismissal of the indictments on the grounds that the prosecution has offered little but conjecture and speculation against my client.'

Judge Morgan then adjourned the trial until the following day, warning the jurors that they must not discuss the case with each other or anybody else while they were away from the courtroom.

18

Judge Morgan's summation, next morning, expounded that crime had been committed, that it appeared the Caulderfield family had bred brothers of questionable morality who did not hesitate in using a gun to suit their ends.

Addressing the jury directly, he said, 'The judge of any court decides on the law, and the jury decides on the facts. But the judge can advise on the facts. The wisdom of twelve minds must differentiate between the probable and the improbable. I believe such facts as have come to light slant the case towards the defendant's guilt. Justice therefore requires that the jury now retires to the jury room and brings in a verdict.'

Brad waited anxiously in a cell beneath the courthouse. Mary-Ellen came to join him and they sat holding hands. Both knew that he had never been closer to the hangman's hand-oiled noose than he was at this moment. Brad hugged his wife in his arms, knowing that her eyes were brimming with tears. He tried to turn their murmurings to the normal things in life and asked, 'How's baby Betsy?'

'She's fine, my love. Annie took her to her own house, has looked after her right well. Annie says she's praying real hard for you. So am I, Brad, every moment of the day.'

Brad swallowed hard, knowing that tears were misting his own eyes. The thought that he might never live to see his little girl grow up had his spirits in his boots.

The court was reconvened after two hours. Many of the spectators had remained in their seats so as not to lose them. When the jury filed back in there was an expectant silence. Brad felt his heart thumping within his chest as he sat next to Wilberforce.

Judge Morgan leaned forward and enquired of the jury if verdicts had been reached. The foreman of the jury answered, 'Yes, Your Honour, unanimously. First charge: the murder of Frank Blevins. Not guilty. Second charge: the murder of Algernon Pike. *Guilty.*'

Brad slumped forward as the courtroom erupted with loud voices and shuffling feet. Mary-Ellen howled with grief. The judge choked off the clamour with a hammering of his gavel, and cried, 'This is a courtroom, not a bawdy house!' He then announced, 'The court is adjourned until two o'clock. It will then be reconvened and I will announce the sentences.'

* * *

She hastened from Austin by rail and stage. She had read of the pending trials in the Austin Gazette. Her remorse had reached fever pitch. She should never have betrayed Brad Caulderfield. She should have kept her love for him locked in her heart. She hoped her nerve would hold and enable her to testify. She also hoped her voice would be strong enough to be heard. It had been a hoarse whisper since she nearly died from strangulation. Even now the bruising remained and was concealed by the scarf she wore.

When Stella Goodnight reached Buffalo Springs she went directly to the attorneys' room in the courthouse and was welcomed by Jock Wilberforce. His jaw dropped in amazement as she related her story; how Pike had left her for dead, and how she had been saved by the prompt action of Sam Makepeace, the saloon proprietor.

At two o'clock the court was reconvened. Brad noticed that Lanny was wheeled into the room. He seemed to have lost all colour in his face. He did not raise his eyes as Judge Morgan made his entry and sat in his high-backed chair.

After a pause, the judge asked Brad

to stand while sentence was read out. However, Wilberforce pressed his hand on Brad's shoulder, preventing him from standing.

The young attorney was on his feet and he said, 'Your Honour. I have a late witness, whose evidence, I believe, will be of the utmost consequence.'

The judge gazed at him, annoyance flaring in his eyes. 'This is most irregular . . . '

'Your Honour, with respect, a man's life is at stake.'

Morgan's face showed a decided flush. 'I know. I know. Call your witness then.'

In a loud voice, Wilberforce cried, 'The defence calls Miss Stella Goodnight.'

Brad could hardly believe his ears, nor indeed his eyes, as Stella was led up the aisle of the courtroom and took her place in the witness chair. She glanced in his direction; their eyes met and the ghost of a smile touched her lips but her attention was drawn away by the

Clerk to the Court who requested her to take the oath. She did this in the faintest of whispers and she was asked to speak up.

Wilberforce stepped forward to question her and his voice was almost joyous. 'Miss Goodnight, what sort of man was Algernon Pike?'

She hesitated, and the courtroom strained to hear. She said, 'He was a murderous man and a bully.'

'Did he ever abuse you?'

'Yes, many times. He often beat me. In Austin he tried to strangle me, but I was saved when my boss, Sam Makepeace, found me.'

The comment brought a buzz of surprise from the court which the judge hammered into silence.

'Did Caulderfield kidnap you?'

'No, I left of my own accord. Brad did not want me to accompany him but I insisted. Had I stayed, Algernon would have strangled me.'

'What was Pike's attitude towards Caulderfield?'

She took a deep tremulous breath. 'He said he would kill me, *just as he would kill Brad Caulderfield.*'

'So you are saying that Algernon Pike had murderous intent towards Caulderfield?'

'Without any doubt.'

Her last response resulted in an uproar in the courtroom, drowning out Wilberforce's, 'I have no more questions, your Honour.'

Judge Morgan's expression settled into a stern scowl. When order had been restored, his words came with due deliberation. 'I will now announce the sentences. Lanny Caulderfield has been found guilty of murder and armed robbery and is sentenced to death by hanging.'

In an unheard-of reaction, a ripple of applause went around the room but quieted as the judge continued to speak. 'The case against Brad Caulderfield, who was charged with the murder of Algernon Pike, is herewith . . . *dismissed.*' And he hammered with his gavel indicating that proceedings were closed. He removed his pince-nez, rose from his chair and left through the doorway at the back.

There followed a turmoil in the courtroom. Everybody was on their feet, milling about. Newsmen rushed out to report their stories. Brad gave Wilberforce's hand a prolonged shake, desperately trying to make his profound gratitude heard above the tumult. Afterwards, he looked towards the witness stand, seeking Stella, but she was gone and he was never to see her again. Mary-Ellen forced her way through the crowd and grasped him in her arms, sobbing with relief that her prayers had been answered.

★　★　★

After his release, Brad rebuilt his father's homestead and moved into it with his family and Annie as house-keeper. He had the remains of his father and Dan Carter transferred to the cemetery in town where formal bury-ings and funerals took place. Brad wrote a letter to Stella, care of the Lucky Strike Saloon in Austin, but received no reply.

In the years that followed the smallholding flourished and in due course became a small ranch. Brad purchased the land from Mulvaney, took into employ four ranch hands, and a busy life blossomed for the Caulder-fields, with the addition of two brothers for Betsy.

Brad's love for Mary-Ellen grew forever deeper and they gradually put the trauma of the past behind them, and cherished their foothold on the earth.

THE END

THE OUTLAW'S DAUGHTER

C. J. Sommers

Matt Holiday is riding a dangerous trail. With $20,000 in missing gold to find and gunfighter Frank Waverly searching for him, it seems unlikely the gold will ever be returned to the Butterfield Stage Company. And the most dangerous gun on the range belongs to the beautiful Serenity Waverly, Frank's daughter. Although she rides with Matt, he suspects that will last only as long as it takes them to recover the stolen gold . . .

IRON EYES THE FEARLESS

Rory Black

Iron Eyes has outgunned the Lucas gang but then discovers that the reward money may not be paid out. Downing most of a bottle of whiskey, Iron Eyes spots another outlaw in the saloon. With time to kill, he allows Joe Kane to run and then sets out after him into forested Indian territory, where he comes under attack. Wounded and tethered to a stake, as triumphant chants echo all around him, he awaits his fate silently. He is unafraid. He is Iron Eyes the Fearless.

GUNS FOR GONZALEZ

Corba Sunman

Captain Slade Moran is tracking three army deserters who have stolen guns and supplies to sell to Mexican bandit, Gonzalez. Time is against Moran, and his situation is about to get even more complicated. The daughter of Gonzalez, fleeing her father's anger, is being pursued by Gonzalez's men, and by breakaway rebel Pedro Sanchez, who wants to use her as a bartering chip against her father. And when the bullets start flying, Captain Moran is right in the middle . . .

RIDE THE SAVAGE RIVER

Scott Connor

Marshal Ellis Moore had been cleaning up Empire Falls for twelve years, but is killed taking on the last of the gun-toters who control his town. At the funeral, Moore's sons learn that he had been on the payroll of Samuel Holdstock, a notorious villain who is now spreading his corrupting influence downriver. Daniel and Henry vow to put right their father's mistakes and deliver Holdstock to justice — a mission even the formidable US Marshal Lincoln thinks is doomed to fail.

THE BLOODSTAINED CROSSING

Matt Laidlaw

In the town of Rawton, a man's death coincides with John Probity's arrival. By the next day another person has died and Probity is in jail, accused of murder. Freed by the enigmatic town barber, Ulysses Court, Probity sets out to discover the truth. With the number of dead rising, Probity and Court witness the gunning-down of some Mexicans at the San Pedro River. Can they make their way to safety and stay one step ahead of the gun-toting outlaws?

THREE DAYS TO ANGEL PASS

Rob Hill

Lucas Redwood makes wrong decisions for the right reasons. A giant of a man, hardly aware of his own strength, he accidentally causes the death of a bullying lumber-camp foreman when he goes to the defence of a friend. Lucas decides to run, but with no money to his name, he becomes involved in a robbery which goes bad. Will this flawed hero evade his pursuers and make it to the border crossing at Angel Pass?